PULP Literature

PULP LITERATURE PRESS

Issue No. 36, Autumn 2022

Publisher: Pulp Literature Press; Managing Editor: Jennifer Landels; Senior Editor: Mel Anastasiou; Acquisitions Editor: Genevieve Wynand; Poetry Editors: Daniel Cowper & Emily Osborne; Assistant Editors: Brooklynn Hook, Veronika Kos, Melisa Gruger; Copy Editor: Amanda Bidnall; Proofreader: Mary Rykov; Graphic Design: Amanda Bidnall; Cover Design: Kate Landels; First Readers: Samantha Olson, Carol McCauley, Jeya Thiessen; Subscriptions: Carol McCauley; Advertising: Brooklynn Hook. For advertising rates, direct inquiries to info@pulpliterature.com.

Cover painting, *The Butterfly Witch* by Melissa Mary Duncan. Artwork for 'Forgive My Delay' by Enrico Orlandi. All other illustrations by Mel Anastasiou.

Pulp Literature: ISSN 2292-2164 (Print), ISSN 2292-2172 (Digital), Issue No. 36, Autumn 2022.

Published quarterly by Pulp Literature Press, 21955 16 Ave, Langley, BC, Canada V2Z 1K5, pulpliterature.com, at $15.00 per copy. Annual subscription $50.00 in Canada, $72.00 in continental USA, $86.00 elsewhere. Printed in Victoria, BC, Canada, by First Choice Books / Victoria Bindery. Copyright © 2022 Pulp Literature Press. All stories and works of art copyright © 2022 their authors as per bylines.

Pulp Literature Press gratefully acknowledges the support of the Canada Council for the Arts.

Pulp Literature is a proud member of the Magazine Association of BC and Magazines Canada.

TABLE OF CONTENTS

FROM THE PULP LIT PULPIT

Daydream Big

Think of a few stations of solitude: a comfy chair beside the fireplace, a well-worn writing table, a cabin window opening onto a pastoral scene. You can practically hear the hush. And with these tableaux come a most delicious thrill for writers and readers alike—the psychological sovereignty to let one's mind drift and wander, come what may.

Ah, the daydream, and its companion question, 'What if?' What if *this* happens? Or what if *that* happens? Or what if—heaven forbid!—*nothing* happens? Because once you begin to answer, you are, by necessity, eliminating countless other possibilities. That first step may be a gesture, but the second is surely a commitment.

And so the pendulum swings: from idleness to activity; from wonder to logic; from mystery to reason. From self to world and back again. If the work of the writer is daydreaming, edited, it is the fortunate reader who receives this daydream at secondhand, invited into their own private reveries.

In both writing and reading, we get to try on other selves. We get to figure out what we are about. Without our daydreams, we are likely to be narrowed to not much more than what the world is commanding us to be. Life may at times feel like a go-along, but, in daydreaming, rebellion escalates.

And so, dear reader, we offer you the daydreams of our writers. They asked, 'What if?' Read on to see how they answered.

~Genevieve Wynand

In THIS ISSUE

Under the wise and watchful gaze of 'The Butterfly Witch' by **Melissa Mary Duncan**, this issue promises that there are at least two sides to every story.

Siblings work through past hurts and begin new journeys in both 'Old Gifts' by feature author **James Sallis** and 'Can-on-a-String' by **Alex Kitt**. Meanwhile, zombies do double duty, bringing a second life to the real-estate market in 'Ambience' by **Jason P Burnham** while offering a message to the living in 'Caught Dead' by **Shawn L Bird**.

We navigate new lands with **Pete Barnstrom** in 'Oeufs Dangereux' and **Cheryl Skory Suma** in 'Adrift off the Shore of Alzheimer Island'. And **Anna Zumbro** in 'The Dump-'Em Dog' and **Mikael Lopez** and **Enrico Orlandi** in 'Forgive My Delay' remind us that, no matter the world in which we live, breaking up is hard to do.

Next, triple your literary delight with historical fiction: 'The Shepherdess: Grandmère Paris' by **JM Landels**, 'Pretty Lies: I Can See for Miles' by **Mel Anastasiou**, and 'Once Upon a Time in Camelot' by **GD Litke**.

And three's the charm for poetry too, with our Magpie Award winners **Cara Waterfall**'s 'griefbody' and 'Harvest' and **Kevin Spenst**'s 'BigGermanDialectWordClankinglyInsertedHere!'.

the adventures of
Allaigna sing

simply a joy to
read

keeps you turning
pages from
beginning to end

An immensely
satisfying epic

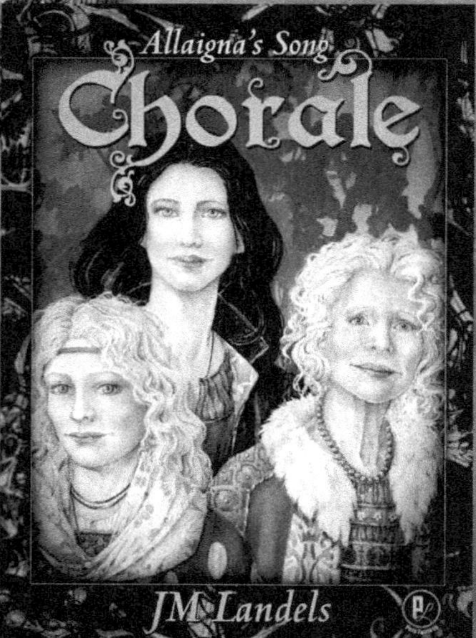

OLD GIFTS

James Sallis

Jim's books include the six volumes of the Lew Griffin cycle, a translation of Raymond Queneau's novel Saint Glinglin, a landmark biography of writer Chester Himes, five collections of poetry, and the source novel for the Cannes-winning film Drive. We were thrilled to receive this superhero story from the renowned crime writer.

Old Gifts

When she was young, which was a long time ago, my mother was a superhero. They'd show her the maps or building plans or whatever, and she'd run over there at close to the speed of sound and save the day. She saved so many days, Dad used to say, they had to add another year onto the calendar.

She and Dad and my teachers, since they were all old too, told me about this. I don't remember any of it because most of it happened before we were born, me and brother Liam. That was when she settled down to take care of us instead of everyone else. We did find her old costume in the back of a closet, with birthday and Christmas presents people gave her still in their boxes. The costume was pink, and shiny like quartz. Moths or something had eaten holes in it.

Twins have the same DNA, right? But Liam got whatever the hero stuff is and I didn't, not a shred of it. He's grown now, both of us are, and he claims he doesn't have anything like that, no stupid damn superpowers, and never did. I'm just like you, he says, just like everyone else. Says he doesn't remember all those nights with the two of us together in our cute little crib that Dad made, me reaching out to grab Liam's leg to keep him from floating up, out, and away. Or how he used to open the window while we lay there across the room, to let the horned owl we considered our pet come in and visit.

Guess we've both floated out and away since. The world's a different place.

When we were seven or eight, not long after we found Mom's old costume, Liam traded his lunch with some kid at school for a sketchbook. Within days it was filled with drawings of our room, our house, the neighbourhood, all of them recognizable but with things subtly off here and there: details, proportions, perspective. Even then I wondered if he was trying to create a duplicate of our world, or another into which he might escape.

Liam's an artist now. And I'm a stern man, a serious man. Oh yes. Maybe you've read my columns on the economy for *The Standard*. Someone must. And while I've no background whatsoever in economics, I do the housework and stable-cleaning required — read what other journalists write, subscribe to a magazine or two, get books from the library and online. But what it mostly amounts to is interviewing authorities on finance and financial institutions, then doing my best to translate what comes out of their mouths into something ordinary folks might understand. A lot of the time, since what they actually say is pretty much gobbledygook, I just make up what I write.

My partner Jeremy loves to read my columns aloud over breakfast, substituting key words with random scientific or religious terms. "The stock market today genuflected toward the Higgs boson, promising redemption just as Shoofly's Theorem foretold" — as I consider sprinkling Sevin Dust on his croissant or adding Goo Gone to his raspberry jam.

Back to Liam, though. In our rare conversations, we never talk about financial matters. Liam's never so much as balanced a chequebook. In all fairness, he doesn't need to. He has agents and accountants and advisors to deal with such. Once, when we were kids, he showed me a painting by Odilon Redon, a lighter-than-air balloon that was in fact a huge eye floating out over the landscape, passenger basket beneath. He loved, he said, the humour of it, the forced second take, the visual pun. Even then it seemed to me a match to some self-image within Liam's own mind.

The closer you look at something, the less it looks like what you first thought.

Tonight it was my turn to cook. I'd planned a salad with butter lettuce, pears, and blue cheese, to be accompanied by omelettes. The first of the omelettes went into the disposal after I grew distracted by Jeremy's discourse on political icons of the fifties. The second one came out near perfect. I slid half onto each plate and set them down by the salad bowls on the kitchen counter, five steps from the dining table we spent months look-ing for, just the right one, and never used. By this time, Jeremy'd stopped talking, either run down or off in the blue, sprinting after some train of thought he'd just missed boarding.

Year after year, as my brother and I grew older and the world grew ever more entangling, we kept waiting for Mom to spring back into action. Checked the box in the closet repeatedly to see if maybe she'd tried on the costume. Listened for lightning-fast footsteps in the backyard, for the sound of her sailing over the chain-link fence. Followed news of the latest storms, disasters, bomb scares, gang wars. Truth to tell, I guess we weren't so much waiting as hoping.

All around us, astonishing things seem to happen, and our lives are so ordinary. We ache for them to be otherwise.

Some of us, anyway. Liam insists that he embraces the world as it is, not some world imagined half into being for its geniality. "Which is why you offer so many variations of it?" I ask.

So many eye balloons floating out over landscapes.

But now that Liam is dying, all those balloons, all those worlds, are about to float up, out, and away for good. And once again we're together here, in this small room, much as we were in our crib as children. If only I could reach out and grab hold of his leg this time.

"I know what this will be like," Liam says. Dying, I suppose he means, but he takes it further. "It will be like flying."

Which is when he tells me.

"That first night, after you left, I felt so alone in the house. You'd gone off to college. Emptiness spilled toward me. Within moments I found myself outside, in dark sky lit by a new moon, sky that looked never to end. I was flying, I was weightless. Free. I've flown every night of my life since."

A nurse comes in then to take vitals and adjust the IV drip at his bedside. Liam thanks her and, when she's gone, goes on.

"Even the comic books we read together as children sought to teach us to question: for what is gained, what is lost? To do this, to go on flying, I had to be alone, stay alone."

This explains so much. I tell him that I understand. That I'm sorry.

"It was not a sacrifice, Joseph," he says. "Never a sacrifice."

And so we wait there together. Wait for one to fly up, out, and away, and for the other's life, any moment now, to come and take him back.

FEATURE INTERVIEW

James Sallis

Pulp Literature: *In 'Old Gifts' we meet a man reflecting on his life, past and present, and on the loss of those he's loved. Could you tell us a bit about the inspiration for this story?*

James Sallis: I was thinking about all that an artist gives up — untold hours of practice on an instrument, years of sitting alone in a room staring at words — for those fleeting moments that click, when the world, for a moment, and just a moment, becomes whole. Also, I'd just reread Carol Emshwiller's wonderful story 'Grandma' and realized this would be a good place to begin: with a family that once, perhaps long ago, had greatness about it. The story assembled itself from those two impulses.

PL: *'Old Gifts' is a lovely braid of both hope and loss — of lift-off and landing. Saying goodbye and letting go is rarely easy. Have you ever had to write or give a eulogy?*

JS: No, but I worked for many years as a critical-care respiratory therapist, initially with adults, then with newborns. I learned a lot about death, about letting go, and about going on living.

PL: *Growing up, was writing, for you, an inevitable calling? At what age did you begin to write?*

JS: The first efforts I remember came when I was about eleven. I typed beginnings of stories on small sheets of note paper, in a voice purloined from Robert Heinlein. Very soon I switched to poems; there were a lot of those, for whom one might blame Robert Frost, ee cummings, TS Eliot, and most especially Edna St Vincent Millay, my first great poet-love. By the time I was fifteen or so, I thought of myself as a writer. I began publishing poems when I was twenty-one, shortly before my first published story, 'Kazoo', appeared in *New Worlds*, the magazine I'd soon help edit. Within weeks, other stories sold — two (the first of many) to Damon Knight for *Orbit*.

PL: *When you were just starting out, how hard was it to break into the publishing world? For better or worse, what do you feel has changed since then?*

JS: There were far fewer people writing then. My submissions had quite a fine chance of being closely considered, and the work, appearing in widely visible and accessible publications, had an excellent chance of getting read. It has never, however, been easy; writers who succeed, then as now, have among whatever artistic gifts they possess, a considerable gift for stubbornness.

While it's true that 'Kazoo' and 'A Few Last Words' sold on their first outings, as of today I have book submissions that have been sitting with prospective publishers for two years. Story submissions regularly camp out on editors' desks for six months or a year before returning with sad feet and a sagging heart to my door.

However, I always like to remind people that my first novel, *The Long-Legged Fly*, which has now appeared in multiple editions here in the States and throughout much of the world and, along with its five companions, in at least four uniform editions, was rejected 36 times before finding a publisher.

PL: *Given this, what advice do you have for new writers beginning to dip their toes into these very crowded literary waters?*

JS: One can only say: Write. Submit. Repeat. And read everything — everything.

PL: *You've written novels, short stories, essays, and poems. How does the writing of each inform the others? Do they take up separate compartments in your writerly brain, or are things more of a literary tossed salad?*

JS: I tend to think of it all — stories, poems, essays, novels, book reviews, criticism — as simply writing. One puts the words and ideas in different containers, whatever might best hold them. I've written a shameless quantity of reviews, well over 130 stories, eighteen or nineteen novels, five collections of poems, a biography of writer Chester Himes; I have edited two books of musicology and translated Raymond Queneau's novel *Saint Glinglin*. Story ideas have become poems, essays have proved fodder for stories … We use what we find in the pantry — and what we trip over as we walk about.

PL: *Have you ever thought about writing a memoir?*

JS: No, though I've done a number of autobiographical essays, most of them published in literary magazines, some collected in *Gently into the Land of the Meateaters*. One essay I've wanted to write for years is an appreciation of the most important single writer in my life, Theodore Sturgeon. Should this ever take form, it will necessarily include a bit of gabble about my early years as a reader and my development as a writer. Sturgeon was the one who most directly led to my becoming a writer, and one I reread again and again, year after year.

PL: *How does research factor into your writing? Have you fallen down any interesting rabbit holes?*

JS: Absolutely, but generally, eventually, I clamber back out. Quicksand was a huge thing in jungle movies when I was a kid; that can be rather what research feels like. You thrash about and just succeed in sinking deeper.

PL: *Are there any writers or poets you turn to again and again?*

JS: Sturgeon, Dylan Thomas, Carol Emshwiller, Patricia Highsmith, Hammett, Samuel R Delany, Edgar Pangborn, James Joyce, Walter Tevis, Blaise Cendrars, Joanna Russ, Alfred Bester, Millay, Marek Hlasko, Boris Vian, Donald Harington, Dorothy B Hughes, Nabokov, Chekhov … How long do you have?

PL: *I'm a little crazy for quotes, and I recently came across this one from Fran Lebowitz: "Contrary to what many of you might imagine, a career in letters is not without its drawbacks — chief among them the unpleasant fact that one is frequently called upon to sit down and write." Does this resonate for you, or are you called every day joyously to the blank page?*

JS: I'll respond with barter. Asked the most difficult part of being a writer, John Updike answered something like, "Getting your butt up the stairs and in the chair."

PL: *What about editing your work? How do you approach this necessary but oh-so-different stage of the writing process?*

JS: I love revision. That, for me, is where the magic seeps in, where voices go clear and where the pages turn from black-and-white to colour.

PL: *Your 2005 novel Drive was the source novel for the Cannes-winning film of the same name. Could you tell us a bit about how that came* *to be? What's it like to see your work come to life in someone else's hands?*

JS: Quite strange and wonderful. One thinks: it's not my novel, and yet—it is! My wife Karyn and I attended the premiere in LA; we may have forgotten to breathe for a time as we watched. It's a great movie. In interviews, I've tagged a story by Donald Barthelme about a being that has a single sexual experience then spends the rest of its life remembering that experience. Nic's movie, for me, was such. I watched it that one time and it's so indelibly etched in my mind that I've never felt a call to see it again.

PL: *Thank you for making the time to speak with us. Before we go, could you tell us, what are you working on now?*

JS: Two novels, one of which is a crime novel about a retired cop-gone-musician returning to his unbeloved hometown;

the other follows two female protagonists in alternate chapters. One's mother was a scream queen in old B-movies, and the other woman hears voices including, perhaps, that of her unborn child. Both precipitously walk away from their jobs and to a great extent their very lives.

Over the past couple of years I've written a dozen or so new stories that have appeared or will soon appear. A sixth poetry collection is, like the boll weevil from the old song, looking for a home.

I'm also at work on the fourth story that eventually will interlink with my novellas *Dayenu*, *Carriers*, *Settlers*, and one or two more to form a book.

SELECTED BIBLIOGRAPHY

NOVELS

The Long-Legged Fly, Avon Books NY, 1994
Moth, Carroll & Graf Publishers, 1993
Black Hornet, Carroll & Graf Publishers,1994
Eye of the Cricket, Walker Books, 1997
Bluebottle, Bloomsbury Press, 1999
Ghost of a Flea, Walker Books, 2001
Death Will Have Your Eyes, St Martin's Press, 1997
Renderings, Black Heron Press, 1995
Drive, Poisoned Pen Press, 2005
Driven, Poisoned Pen Press, 2012
Cypress Grove, Walker Books, 2004
Cripple Creek, Walker Books, 2006
Salt River, Walker Books, 2007
What You Have Left: The Turner Trilogy, Walker & Company, 2009
The Killer Is Dying, Walker & Company, 2011
Others of My Kind, Bloomsbury USA, 2013
Willnot, Bloomsbury USA, 2016
Sarah Jane, Soho Crime, 2019

AS EDITOR

Ash of Stars: On the Writing of Samuel R Delany, University Press of
  Mississippi, 1996
Jazz Guitars, University of Nebraska Press, 1996
The Guitar in Jazz, University of Nebraska Press, 1996

Non-fiction

The Guitar Players, HarperCollins Publishers, 1982
Difficult Lives, Gryphon Books, 1993
Saint Glinglin by Raymond Queneau (translator), Dalkey Archive, 1993, 2000
Gently into the Land of the Meateaters, Black Heron Press, 2000
Chester Himes: A Life, Walker Books, 2000
A James Sallis Reader, Point Blank, 2005
Difficult Lives / Hitching Rides, Gryphon Books, 1993

"The conjugal blend of mystery and Hollywood atmosphere works on every level. Very highly recommended."

PULPLITERATURE.COM/THE-EXTRA-A-MONUMENT-STUDIOS-MYSTERY

PRETTY LIES: I CAN SEE FOR MILES

Mel Anastasiou

Mel Anastasiou is a novel acquisitions and story editor with Pulp Literature Press, and she co-founded Pulp Literature *magazine* in 2013. Mel helps writers develop through her structural editing, the popular 'Writing Muse' Twitter feed, and two workbooks, The Writer's Boon Companion: Thirty Days Towards an Extraordinary Volume *and* The Writer's Friend and Confidante: Thirty Days of Narrative Achievement. *Her fiction includes the Hertfordshire Pub Mysteries, the Monument Studio Mysteries, and the Stella Ryman Mysteries, for which she won a Literary Titan Gold book award and was longlisted for the Leacock Medal.*

$\mathcal{I}$ Can See for Miles

It's the sun-drenched summer of 1974 on Bowen Island, BC. Inspired by the story of Orpheus and Euridice, Jenny Riley searches for re-entry into the ghost world to bring back her dead love, Joey. These attempts put her and others in mortal danger, and Jenny's search is increasingly threatened by the ghost of Moira, who presses upon Jenny her own reckless agenda for life after death.

Chapter 21

Nobody could stay alive under water this long.

Jenny hung somewhere between the surface and the depths, her struggles squeezed out of her by Moira's strong hands. She was drowning. Possibly, she was already drowned. She couldn't remember when she'd last breathed. And, as she'd already established, no one could hang halfway between the seabed and the surface this long.

Although, if her lungs were filled with water, wouldn't she sink?

She was so cold that she couldn't feel the water. *Hold on,* she told herself. *Just a little longer.* She'd said those words to Joey in the steaming wreck of the car. *Help is coming.* And help had come, but by then Joey was already dead in the front seat of the yellow Zed.

"If it comes too late, can you even call it *help?*" she whispered. A bubble of air tickled her lips as it escaped, touched her nose, and rose away from her. She wondered whether her next thought might be her last, and so she thought about Joey—about herself and Joey, when they were small and daring, perched facing one another on their next-door windowsills, small feet dangling far above the ground. They used to push their thumbs against their eyelids, calling out the colours they saw exploding in their eyeballs. She saw them now against her lids. She murmured, "I see swirls of colour, red more than anything, red everywhere, and flashing blue …"

Moira said, "*I* see white. I always see white, like a wedding veil."

"White like seagulls." This was quite a ghost world, where she could speak and hear underwater. Jenny pictured her words floating from her mouth in small silver bubbles, up to the surface of the Sound.

Moira's hands loosened a little. "Like whitecaps on the water."

"Like the sides of a great white ship, when you jump off it."

"Shut up." Moira pinched her.

"Or what? Or you'll drown me?" Jenny's mouth curled upwards. Maybe irony was the last emotion she would feel. She would float away from life in the arms of an ironic thought, held underwater by a dead woman. If a person could die in the world where dead people lived.

"I love Joey. But I kissed Malcolm. That's ironic, too." Jenny's heart had chosen for her, because her heart had never learned to love anyone but Joey. "I think I kissed Malcolm because he's alive. It's harder to love Joey when he's dead."

"Love is a mystery," Moira said. "Your heart chooses, and it's like a law somebody made. We have to do what it says."

Jenny opened her eyes at last and got what she least expected: a bit of luck. An eddy caught Moira's hair and swirled it in front of her face so that she let go of Jenny to push it back. Freed, Jenny found some unexpected strength, enough to push Moira away. It was like pushing the cool, slick stems of floating kelp. She looked upwards. The surface seemed impossibly distant.

Whether she was dead or alive, she'd push up out of the water into the open air, even if her arms and legs gave out. Even if it meant leaving her body behind her to do it.

The blue and green dappled surface grew no closer. She might indeed have to shuck off her body, leaving her old flesh-and-bone self here to drift away into the depths like an empty white shell so that she, the essence of Jenny, could rise. She almost laughed to think how confounded Moira would be, confronted with Jenny's empty, dead body. Moira was clever in her way, but she lacked a certain awareness.

Jenny kicked at the water. Once, twice, and that was all she had inside her. In another moment her body would fall into the darkness to lie with the fish and the rocks, with the running shoes she'd dropped out of the rowboat a couple of days earlier. Two white canvas shoes, bought not so long ago for a dollar forty-nine at Woodward's department store, the pair of them moving side by side in the deepest currents of the Sound. Her body would touch down near them, and after a while barnacles would adhere to her bones. While she, the drowned but unkillable Jenny spirit, would leap up through the waves like a fish.

The thought so cheered her that she summoned the will to scissor her legs and kick upwards again. The sun beamed hard against the surface, and she recalled her sunlit march across Bowen Island with Malcolm and Adrian, and how the little boys sprouted out in song and puffed their strong young bodies along the forest path. She remembered again the hard line of Malcolm's mouth when he'd kissed her.

She felt she ought to do *something* for those she was leaving behind. One more kick upwards for Malcolm, and one for her sister Rachel. One more kick for Frances, with her Swiss-knife honesty. And that was it. That was all she had in her. All she could do now was slide out of flesh and bone, hair and skin, down through the slippery sea. And, since it was most likely to be her last moment of life, Jenny felt it incumbent to open her eyes. With a crash of light, she broke through the surface.

She was too surprised to remember to breathe, but her body breathed for her, and a poor job it did of it, with razor breaths and coughs that took in salt water and forced it up her nose. She pumped a great gulping breath that went a little way towards restarting the living engine inside her.

She rested at the surface. Waves slapped and rolled around her. Sunlight flashing on the water nearly blinded her to everything but glimpses of blue sky.

"The shore," she croaked, just to see if she could, "must be attainable." She wasn't so sure, though.

She cast about for a directional clue among the swelling waves and caught sight of trees and a bluff rising up from the water. She turned towards them, but when she attempted a breast stroke, her outstretched hands touched something smooth and cold. She jerked her hands away, certain that she had found Moira in the water, but it was only a seal, brown as deadwood, floating on the surface. Its dark eyes gazed at her from under hairy brows.

She and the seal bobbed up and down with the waves, while the sun flashed and bounced upon the water.

She was a strong swimmer, but how long could she stay afloat?

"I'm exhausted. That's bad …" She coughed and drew a great long wheeze into her lungs. The seal watched her. "But I'm young. And the water temperature is bearable." She wasn't sure what she could tell a seal about sea water that it didn't already know. In summer, the top few feet of water were cool but not bitter. Still, it occurred to her she wouldn't be able to tread water forever.

She felt something smooth brush across her ankles. Kelp? She kicked again, and felt cold fatigue return to her limbs. She concentrated on gratitude for the sun's heat on her forehead.

"A friend told me once that the human species begins to die …" A wave washed across her face and she blew the water out of her nose. "He told me that people begin to die at the cellular level at the age of eighteen. So it's all downhill from there."

The seal sank beneath the surface and Jenny was glad it had, because now she could stop acting as if she were brave. And, should she sink after all, she would not want the seal to follow her down, holding her with that wet dark gaze, watching her like a television show while she drowned. And what if—while her eyes glazed over—what if the seal's round face grew pale and the dark eyes turned grape green and those white fingers reached out for her again? She treaded water hard until her arms and legs stopped on their own and she rested, lips and nose and mouth just out of the water, just for a moment. Either way, just for a moment.

She heard the whirring noise again. She smelled gasoline. A boat must be nearby. But how would its driver or passengers see her as she floated low in the water—just two eyes, two lips, and a nose on the glittering surface of the sea? And even those would be hidden with every rise and fall of the waves.

Something bumped her shoulder, something hard and gently curved. She raised a palm and it skidded against the side of a boat. Not a big boat, but she didn't need a big boat. Nor did the temperature of the water matter any longer, or the fatigue in her limbs. She slapped both hands against the boat, reaching up towards the gunwales, which were well out of reach. Someone had better hear her soon, because if the boat started moving again, so would the propeller. If you got caught in the blades, wouldn't it be like being eaten by sharks? Taking a first bite of you, your feet perhaps, while the rest of you screamed in brief and bloody protest.

A man's hand reached down and took hold of her wrist. She strained to reach up the side of the boat, kicking her way up towards the gunwales, helping her rescuer as best she could. He had her by her wrists now, and the weight of her own body and the pull of the water were nearly unbearable.

And now, an added pull against her rescuer: something closed around Jenny's left ankle, just below the surface. Even weary, even striving, she counted four fingers and a thumb taking hold of her ankle. *Moira.* But strong arms won out and hauled her up and over into the well of the boat. She banged her knees and shins on cleats as she fell. A man gathered her into his arms and held her close, her back against his chest. Her head was turned at such an angle that all she could see was the side of the small boat's canopy, and the water beyond — empty, but for a great white ferryboat chugging up the coast. She could hear the purser's voice over the speakers, blaring a warning at another small boat crossing its bow.

"Ssh," the man whispered.

He held her tightly. There was a familiar, unpleasant smell to him. All she could see of him was his wrist, and the pale hairs along it, like Joey's wrists. And, above that, the arm of Lerner's waxed canvas jacket.

"You're all right now," he said.

Jenny hit him. She kicked him and pushed at his chest. She would not—would never again—go where Lerner's kiss would take her.

Under her pounding fists, Lerner's waxed canvas jacket seemed to give off an increasing stench. Her wet shirt clung to his jacket, as if she belonged there.

She bit his thumb and spat at the taste of him. "Let me go. I swear I'll kill you."

He crushed her against him. His chest shook against her cheek, as if he were laughing, but she knew Lerner's laugh, and this was not it. Lerner's laugh was a bark like a battered dog's.

Tears streamed down her cheeks.

"Jenny, please."

By this point, Jenny wasn't entirely sure whether she was dead or alive—asleep, dreaming, or drowned—but she was certain of this voice. She would know it anywhere: at sea, on the moon, or in the depths of a dark garage.

She choked out, "You smell like Lerner."

Joey laughed again. "I'm wearing his jacket, that's all. I always liked his jacket, didn't you?"

Joey let her go, and she collapsed against the side of the boat. When she looked up, he stood at the speedboat's steering wheel, looking out across the bow. She saw his hand move to the throttle. As he shoved it forward, Jenny seized the back of the passenger seat and held on tight.

He shouted, "Speedboat dashboards are a lot like car dashboards, aren't they? Even the windshields, although the wheel's on the wrong side. Why would the wheel of a boat be on the wrong side? This isn't England."

Jenny struggled to hold herself steady against the pitching of the boat. Her clothes were soaking and clung to her. "The right side is the wrong side, Joey."

"That's my Jenny, the girl with the corkscrew mind."

Jenny blew out a breath. She pulled herself forward and seized the top of the windshield with both hands to stand next to him. She took in the sight of his familiar, handsome profile. She'd not seen it since just after he'd crashed that yellow Zed into the telephone pole. Just after he'd died, and she'd lived.

The wind blew spray into the boat, and he wiped his face with one hand.

Jenny said, "Joey, take off that jacket."

"Soon. I've got to keep my eye on the road."

"What *road*? We're at sea." She was so happy to see him that she seemed to be drying her clothes from the inside out. So happy that she'd argue with him all day and into the night. "Throw that jacket overboard, Joey."

"Is that where you think we are? At sea?"

The boat bucked as a wave hit it sideways, and she ducked too late to avoid the spray. She climbed up onto the seat behind him and put her arms around him.

"Can I stay in this place, wherever it is?" *Wherever you are*, she wanted to add, but it sounded like a Supremes lyric, and anyway she knew Joey better than to spoil a moment with too much love.

The boat bumped its bottom on a wave, and the canvas shoulder of Lerner's jacket moved against her breast. "Beautiful British

Columbia, where by rain or at sea you'll always end up soaked to the skin." Joey's tone was light, but he shivered. She wondered what in heaven or on earth he could possibly be afraid of. He was dead.

She'd go into that another day.

"You came to my rescue," she said. "I feel like the prince in The *Little Mermaid,* saved from a watery grave."

Joey snorted. "I'm always coming to your rescue."

This was an untrue statement. From Joey, who never lied. Impossible. He must be joking.

"When else did you ever rescue me?" Jenny asked lightly. She was always rescuing *him.* But she remembered finding herself trapped in a dark room in Lerner's house — was it the bathroom? She remembered the smell of the toilet. And a lot of pushing and waxed-canvas-smelling warmth. She with leaden arms, having drunk the drink in the green glass. Lerner mumbling and physically stronger than she would ever have believed, until Joey banged the door open so that it caught Lerner on the head, and everything that was happening in the little room stopped. "At the party. You saved me then, too. Lerner was …" She couldn't go on.

"You were asking for it, going in there with him. But I didn't let that stop me from pulling you out." Joey shrugged. "See, I'm not such a bad guy after all."

"I never said you were. Who said you were?"

He didn't answer. He grinned like a pirate and jerked at the wheel to quarter a series of large waves.

Jenny held on tight. Through her teeth — clenched, so that she wouldn't bite her tongue — she said, "Darling Joey, you need to adjust the tilt of the boat so it won't bump so hard."

"Darling Jenny, shut up."

"Damn it, Joey. Stop the boat! I need you to turn off the engine right now."

She felt his sigh more than heard it. He pulled back on the throttle. The little speedboat rocked as its engine idled unevenly.

Joey left the wheel and sat on the floor in the middle of the boat with his back propped against the passenger seat. She slipped down beside him in the centre of the boat. "Now take that thing off," she said. "Please."

He wriggled out of Lerner's jacket, dropped it over the side, and pulled her up against his chest. "There. Happy? Don't spoil it."

"Okay," she lied, because she planned to spoil it. How could she not? There had never been another way to get what she wanted from him. But for now, let this be enough: to pillow her head on his chest while his kiss bumbled about like a dragonfly on the top of her head. She gazed upwards into a perfect blue sky. It was almost too perfect to be true. Was this boat in the ghost world, or the world of the living? Maybe, when Moira tried to drown her, and Jenny had stopped caring whether she lived or died, she had accidentally found the way through some crack in the wall between life and death. Furthermore, if they were back in the world of the living, then she might already have succeeded in bringing Joey back to life. She felt a pang of guilt at the thought of such a success. Why should she alone bring her loved one back to life, when the rest of the world mourned its dead and moved on?

That seemed a problem for the ages. A more practical question was, where in heaven or hell had Joey procured a speedboat? The impossibility of answering that question in any sensible way was enough to break her heart with worry that they were still in the ghost world after all.

Something slapped at the side of the boat. Jenny felt Joey strain against her to look over the gunwale.

She asked, "What is it?"

"Nothing. Just keeping alert in case you need more saving." He laughed down at her.

When she shivered, he pulled her tighter, still laughing. The night he crashed the yellow Zed, Joey had laughed at her, driving towards home. He often laughed at her, but he never drove. He never got his licence. He refused to risk DUI. When her sister said Joey was lazy, Jenny said Joey was a lot of things, but he didn't lie, and he didn't drive.

Except the night she was so tanked by the drink in the green glass. Except the night he died.

She felt him shift so that the top of her head was under the point of his chin. The pressure was uncomfortable. But she worked hard not to care about anything except the living touch of her dead love, and their reunion here, under what seemed like the same sky she'd left behind on the mainland. If this were still the ghost world, it looked exactly like the ordinary world, where it mattered what you ate and who called you on the phone. The sea was the same deep blue-green around the boat, and the shoulders of land rose out of the same Sound. Sunlight broke a trail across the waves. A trail Moira could walk. And maybe Joey, too.

Jenny wondered whether she'd misunderstood about the ghost world. Maybe it was not a separate place, but the same world she'd always known. They might still be in it, invisible to living people. But if the dead shared the same world with the living — shared the ocean and sky, and all these forests — wouldn't the same rules of nature apply?

But Moira could walk across water.

Jenny pushed that thought aside and pulled Joey's arm tighter around her. She raised her face to the sun. Maybe this was as happy as you got in this place. It would certainly do, for now.

She heard another heavy splash.

Joey sat up straight so that Jenny almost fell over. "Did you hear that?"

"It was only a seal." Jenny sat up.

"Now, listen to me. You know what happened that night at the party?" He sounded distracted.

"You saved me."

He patted her shoulder. "Good. Remember that. No matter what happens, hold on to that: *I saved you because I love you.*"

In all the years she'd known him, he had never said *I love you.* The words sent the blood bubbling through her.

Taking his hand, she held it up, and the sun shone through it as it would shine through a porcelain cup. He tugged his hand out of hers.

"Shit," he whispered, getting to his knees. Then, "*Allrightallrightallright.*"

She pulled on his arm. "Who are you talking to?"

"Nobody. Myself." He scrambled into the driver's seat. The roar of the engine rose and then softened as the boat moved forward. The wind lifted his hair as he drove, one palm flat on the throttle. "Look, you should maybe go back home now. Get out of here. It's not safe."

"Nothing's safe." Jenny would have told a thousand lies to keep him, but for once the truth was good enough. "And I don't even know how to go back."

"Well, you sure don't want to go where I'm going."

But she couldn't mistake the gleam in his eye. She'd known Joey all her life, and she saw now that he was glad she wanted to come with him. Possibly he even thought he'd manipulated her into coming. As if he needed to.

"I always follow you, Joey. Together forever, isn't that what we said?"

"And we sealed it in blood." He gave her shoulder a squeeze and added, "I'll have to floor it before she comes back."

Jenny didn't ask who. She climbed up beside him and looked over the side of the boat. A head broke the water, but it was only another seal, gazing after them with wet dark eyes. Joey pushed the throttle forward, and Jenny bit her tongue.

The little speedboat planed the waves, the hills rising as green as Middle-earth beside the shining water. Ahead she saw the white mass of another ferryboat heading north for Bowen Island.

If the ferry captain could see them, he'd sound his horn to warn them off. She didn't care. She only cared about Joey, and the way he stood so tall, like a bold and fictional mariner, resting one hand on the steering wheel. His arm held her close to his chest, and she gripped him tighter, gripped him until he laughed and pulled at her hand.

She said, "Don't go too close to the ferryboat."

"What ferryboat?"

He was right. They were not on a speedboat tearing up Howe Sound, racing towards a ferryboat in brilliant sunshine. Instead, they were on a dark road, in the Zed, and Joey had the wheel. But it didn't matter, as long as she could hold on to this moment. "Don't leave me behind."

"Of course I won't leave you." He leaned forward as the road tore past.

Jenny said, "Nothing as bad as that crash can happen twice."

"Everything happens just once," Joey said. "Once, or an infinite number of times."

"No, everything happens in opposing pairs," Jenny argued. "Black or white. In or out. Up or down. There are always alternatives, Joey."

It would be all right, as long as they were together.

"Dead or alive," Jenny added. She closed her eyes. "Yes or no."

"Yes." Joey laughed and took a left turn at high speed. "Always yes, Jenny."

Chapter 22

Frances was forced to call upon a lifetime's amassed professorial authority in order to wangle the three little boys out of the water and onto the beach, and then, of course, they were wet. So was she. Back at her house, she fussed the children into some of her spare clothes and gave them their own soggy shorts and T-shirts in plastic bread bags. There were complaints about wearing girls' clothes, and about the breadcrumbs in the bottoms of the bags. Then she hurried them out the back door and down the road towards the cove.

"Can't you slow down?" the kids asked.

"I could, but then I'd be late."

"For what?"

"For the ferry."

"Then what?" Tanaka asked.

Frances didn't answer. She was operating on her instinct that Jenny was in need of her help, so there was nothing sensible she could tell them, and she didn't want to make anything up. They were such appalling little liars that only the truth should be told to them.

"The police are going to arrest you for making us wear these stupid girls' clothes," Two-Can growled.

"They're *my* clothes," Frances snapped, "and I want them back. *Ironed.* And where are your clothes I gave you? Where are the bread bags?" They had thrown them into the bushes, she supposed. Well, she wasn't going to look for them. They could wear girls' clothes forever, as far as she was concerned. "You are free to hate girls' clothes all you want."

"I like them," Tanaka said sarcastically. "I like wearing women's underwear."

"I'm wearing a bra," Flash bragged. Of course he wasn't.

Lying, swearing, and singing at her heels, Flash, Two-Can, and Tanaka ran with her towards the cove and the next ferry sailing. They tore over the top of the hill and down the other side, past the general store, towards the ferry landing. The ferryboat was just in. Timing would be tight, but Frances had a chance to make the sailing.

Except … *Hell take these untimely children.* But was there ever a child who worked to anyone's convenience? She tried to imagine her archaeological rival Gig Chalmers as a child, but couldn't get past his sideburns.

Her shoes slipped on the gravel at the side of the road. She stopped and turned to the boys. "Look, the three of you wait at the store. When I get to the other side, I'll phone somebody at the camp to pick you up there."

Two-Can met her gaze evenly. "Sure. Just give us kids some money."

Frances threw him a crumpled dollar bill from her shorts pocket and ran down the hill. She hadn't run in a while, not since she'd tried jogging for a week after her forty-ninth birthday. Today running felt good, especially on the downhill, except for the pain on the outside of her knee. And she felt better knowing the kids were waiting safely at the store.

Little feet pattered behind her, but the cars were nearly unloaded, so she didn't dare stop, not even in order to tell the kids to turn back. Instead she ran faster, trusting the ratio of her leg length against theirs. But still the feet followed her, three pairs of soft-soled shoes flapping against the gravel at the side of the road.

"*You can't love four and fit through the door,*" Tanaka puffed as he pulled past her, the other two at his heels.

"If you're shorter, you should be slower," she grunted. Car after car passed them, heading uphill, fresh off the ferry.

"*You can't love eight and still see straight,*" Flash shouted as he ran past.

"Damn your eyes, don't you know how to count?" Frances sped up. It was amazing how you thought you had these young children handled, you thought you were in control, and then *presto!* Anarchy. Give her university students any day, all serious in their corduroys. Even better, give her shards of ancient pots and broken tiles, quiet mornings with dead bones and cups of strong tea.

"That's your car on the ferryboat, Frances." Flash reached the dock rail first and pointed towards the ferry deck. "The old green piece of crap Galaxie. I remember."

"Watch your language," she told him, but she was so glad to see her car that she was hard put to sound severe. The Galaxie sat at the end of the line, behind a yellow Gremlin, and she thought it would be last to unload. The Gremlin drove off the ship and up the ramp, but the Galaxie didn't move from its spot. A young ferry officer waved it off, but there was nothing doing. Was the battery dead? That happened sometimes. In a moment, Jenny would get out—or that boy, Malcolm. Or both of them, probably, to look for help from the ferry crew.

But no one got out. The car sat on the ferry deck in the afternoon sun, blank and baking.

The ferry officer strode across the deck and banged the flat of his hand on the Galaxie's hood. Frances ran out onto the dock, took hold of the top of a nearby piling, and leaned out to see what was going on. Her hand slipped on the piling and she dug her fingers into a crack in the side. She didn't want to fall off the dock into the oil-slick waters below. She remembered back to when she was as young as Tanaka, Two-Can, and Flash were now, when men used to jump from the pilings into the water behind the cruise ship. How they tossed and shouted in the foam behind the ship as her mother held her by her bunched-up shirt, cautioning her that it was a long way down, that you could bump your head on the tarred pilings. She remembered how the women watching cheered, smiled, and fixed their hair while the men scrambled to shore.

The young ferry officer slapped his hand on the Galaxie's hood again. He looked inside the car and shook his head. Then he made a wide-armed gesture towards the front of the ship, and the cars waiting in line to board began filing onto the ramp that led to the car deck. The Galaxie sat in the corner as if left to be junked.

"Damn it." Frances ran back to the loading ramp, the kids at her heels.

I don't want them. "Come on," she told them. It was strictly forbidden to board as a foot passenger when the cars were loading, but stragglers could board afterwards. The little boys ran up the stairs towards the lounge level, while down on the car deck Frances strode between the lines of parked vehicles towards the Galaxie. She hoped Jenny was all right. If so, Frances would enjoy giving her hell about driving the car.

CHAPTER 23

Here at the wheel of the yellow 240 Z, Joey had never felt luckier. He'd fallen in love at last with his Jenny, after all the years of keeping his emotional cool. To celebrate his lovestruck status, he stepped harder on the gas. He took a curve that would have sent Jenny's dad's VW hatchback flying into the bushes. But the Zed was a beauty, and it hugged the road.

In the passenger seat beside him, Jenny sat buckled up tight with her eyes closed and her hair fanned across her face. She was usually so alert. And she was always the one at the wheel. He laughed, although not at Jenny. Joey laughed aloud because Robin Hood laughed as he leapt from the parapet with Maid Marian in his arms; because the Sundance Kid laughed all the way down the cliff to the water below — or did the Kid swear? His fellow outlaws, riding high, like him. And he was further gifted today with the certainty that saving Jenny paid for all.

He couldn't remember ever feeling this happy, at least not when he was sober. Strange, that he couldn't remember how he'd come to be in this usually inadvisable condition. When you're drinking, you want value for money — that was his joke. The way he said it, he always got a laugh from the boys. But tonight he appreciated for the first time how good it felt to be steady and sober. To be solid at the wheel, his reactions like James Bond's. He laughed again as the trees whipped by outside the car.

He'd rescued Jenny! And had fallen in love with her. Should he tell her so again? Maybe not yet. For one thing, you didn't want to give a girl too much power over you. Like the Ancient Greeks used to say, *moderation in everything.*

Furthermore, he knew she'd loved him for years. So telling her again now might raise the question of exactly what he'd been feeling towards her throughout their long, intertwining past. He did not want to explain the difference between the old, hard necessity of keeping her around and this new, true romantic love.

Jenny stirred and coughed. "Oh, God, Joey. Why of all places are we in your father's Zed?"

"Why not, I'd like to know?" He glanced at her. She was okay, even after that drink he made her in the green glass. She was white as a ghost, but okay. And so was he. Joey could hear the future calling him, clear as a good FM radio signal. "I'm going to sober up. No more drinking, no more little coloured pills. I like me like this."

"You said that at Christmas."

"That was the old me and the old you." Joey shot her a humorous look. "I'm going to drink milk and give coins to charity. I'm going to speak to teen audiences on the dangers of drugs and the brown snub bottle."

"*I'm* going to puke," Jenny said.

He caught the gleam of an amber light up ahead and double-geared down to take the corner. The world didn't know what a good driver he was, but the world would soon learn. He took the corner perfectly, looked at Jenny, and winked.

"Don't look at me, for God's sake. Watch where you're going. You'll crash."

"Promises, promises," Joey said. "You just take your rest, my rescued damsel. You just let me drive you home."

"You never even bothered to get your licence. You don't *drive*." She undid her seat belt and bent over, resting her head on the glove box door. He heard her spit on the floor of the car. Well, the Zed had seen worse. He would get the car detailed, and then they could all be particular.

He smiled down at her and shook his head. *Me! In love!* He'd never thought it would happen. But tonight marked a change. He'd get his licence and he'd sober up. Girls would turn around to watch him drive by. *Guys* would turn around to watch him take a corner. He took one now, and then another, faster. He grinned as he heard her roll down the window, and the wet noise that meant Jenny was throwing up.

"Nice one," Joey said without irony. "Hang on, not much longer."

The car roared, and he heard the wet sound again.

"Oh, god." She rolled up the window and put her seat belt back on. "I had cola, that's all. You know that's all. A green glass full of cola."

He didn't answer.

"I'm sure there was something else slipped into it."

"Yeah, I guess so." He snorted and pulled up, the Zed's nose just sniffing at the stop line at the red light at Lonsdale and Third. He peered through the windscreen at the Vancouver lights across the Narrows. "That drink was going to happen at some point, Shirley Temple. And you have to learn how to handle yourself when you're out of control. But never mind. I rescued you from Lerner, and here I am, driving you safely home."

The light changed, and he felt the car jerk forward as he shifted into first. He was a better driver than that, though—rusty, was all. He'd get his licence first time out. He'd go tomorrow, probably get that young testing guy the kids used to talk about a couple of years ago when his contemporaries were getting their licences. The testing guy was tough but fair. The excellent thing about getting your licence a few years late was that you were not easily shaken. You were more certain of yourself physically. Joey pictured the moment at the end of the driving test. The testing guy would shake his hand and say Joey was the best he'd ever seen.

He heard Jenny swear. He said, "You must be feeling better."

"I think it must have been your bloody friend Lerner who put something in my cola. How can I change what happened that night? How can I help you if I can't even sit up?"

"Tonight *I'm* helping *you*," Joey said. "Shut up and enjoy." The car bumped up on the curb—it was a low curb, invisible in the night, and that could happen to anyone. He slowed down a little and wished she'd get off the subject. That drink he'd concocted for her had been a mistake, that was all. Anybody could make a mistake. Let Lerner take the blame. Lerner would be cool with it.

Jenny said, "It had to be Lerner who made the drink. Or one of those other …"

"Not now!" Shit. That was a flashing cop light in the distance. The North Shore was over-patrolled. He sped up again, and something gleamed right in front of the car. Eyes in the night.

Joey shouted, a wordless cry that knocked him backwards against his seat.

Then, "Jenny, did you see it? A deer. A damn, stupid deer. What is it tonight? Is everything out to—"

"Slow down, can't you?"

"Double shit. There's someone on the road."

He slammed on the brakes. As the car swerved to a stop, he saw nothing but streetlights shining through black trees and on sleeping houses, the roofs dark grey and blank like unplugged TVs. He rested his elbows on the wheel and caught his breath. At the driver's side window, two palms pressed up against the glass.

Beyond the hands, two eyes green as a cat's in the night gazed in at them.

He heard Jenny whisper, "Moira ..."

"I'm not stopping for *her*." Joey's Adam's apple rose and fell as he wrenched the car into gear and moved ahead.

Out of the corner of his eye he saw pale hands drag across his window. He sped up to leave Moira behind them and checked the rear-view. He saw nothing there but the reflection of the crumpled red-and-green Mexican blanket on the Zed's back-seat ledge.

"We're not really here, Joey," Jenny murmured. "You know we're not. We already did this night. If I can't change things, I don't want to do it again. Why can't we be together in the best parts? Like the time we went camping and left Rachel in the woods? Why does it have to be the worst part?"

He frowned. "Driving you home tonight, safe and sound, *is* the best part."

"Or couldn't we just be playing together when we were little? Remember? Cooties and Tonka trucks, and Chatty Cathy hung by one foot for weeks out the window. "

"Tonka toy trucks, yeah. Still got them. You know what's funny? I hid my weed stash in the cement mixer." He grinned. "This isn't the worst part, Jenny. How could it be? I love this car. I love *you*." There, he'd said it again! Easier than he'd ever have believed. He held his breath, waiting for her to reply. Goddam Malcolm was the wild card, and it pissed Joey off that he wasn't certain how she'd answer.

"I love you, too," she said.

Joey grinned. *Take that, Malcolm.* He'd been right to tell her after all. So, he said it again and again in the darkness, right up to the moment when he saw ahead of them the vertical slash of the telephone pole, a second before they hit it.

He braced himself, and in the blackness before they hit, there was a swift but clear moment when he wished he'd worn a seat belt. After that came a sound like the world ending. He slammed forward against the wheel, against the back of his seat, and forward again. It was all so quick. And then so quiet.

A guy had time to think when it was quiet.

He would have turned his head, but his neck hurt. As well, there was something wrong with his eyes, and his arms wouldn't move. He lay where he was, his head back against the seat of the Zed, listening to something liquid pour out onto the road underneath them.

In the still air, he smelled gasoline and something acrid … something acid. He heard Jenny's intake of breath. He heard her say his name, and then—she had always amazed him, even though he never let on—he felt a light touch at his right temple. He let out a long breath and wondered why nothing hurt.

His right eye gained a sort of swimming focus and caught the dart of a shadow outside. Here, then gone. The policeman. It had to be the policeman.

"Oh, *this* is it," he said. He'd know this moment anywhere. "*Now* it's the worst part."

Chapter 24

"Are you okay?" Joey's voice sounded as if it had crawled out of his mouth and across the space that separated their seats to reach her.

Jenny was afraid to exhale, but her body did it for her. Then — which hurt more, her arm or her leg? — she slowly inhaled again. She pushed at her door, but it wouldn't move. *Remember, after the Zed crashed, the passenger door had to be opened from the outside.* Letting go the handle, she lay back and sucked salt from her upper lip.

"No, I'm not okay."

"We're both alive. Right, Jenny?"

"Alive. Yes."

He shifted slightly in the seat beside her.

"Jenny, we've still got a minute or two before we die. I can feel it, can't you?"

The shattered windshield offered no reflections. She would have to turn her head to look at him. It seemed like nothing inside her body was working as it should. But she wasn't dead. She and Joey were still together, still conscious. As before, he would die and she would live, unless somehow she could change things here in the ghost world. She remembered the policeman and the wrenching sound of the car door as he levered it open. The shudder of metal and springs underneath her. She remembered the nurses and a doctor with a nasty little moustache but kind eyes. Her sister Rachel, her visitor's chair pulled up tight against the hospital bed, urging Jenny to open her eyes and speak to her. Rachel reciting *Desiderata* and pinching Jenny's uninjured arm to make her talk.

Now Jenny said aloud the words that Rachel had quoted to comfort her, as nearly as she could remember them. *"Don't distress yourself with terrible imaginings."*

Joey laughed. "So we're imagining this, are we? And imagining that there's nothing wrong with you except a deep bruise on the thigh and a slice down the inside of your arm?"

"Be quiet just a moment, Joey. I'm trying to think." There had to be a way to change what seemed to be happening, or else why was she here?

Something dark fluttered against the window.

She heard Joey cough, a hollow, damp sound. She managed to move her head a little to get a proper look at him. Blood inked his blond hair. She heard him say, "You must see it by now, Jenny. The dying see the dead."

"I only see you," she answered. "We have to leave the ghost world, Joey. You have to come with me back to the real world. Like Orpheus, remember? I'm going to walk out of Hades and take you with me."

Joey took a deep sigh. It sounded like a last breath. "Poor Jenny! Nothing is that easy."

"This is my chance to save you," she whispered. Her throat hurt, and she took a moment to swallow the bitter taste on her tongue. She had cut her arm somehow, and she made out the early signs of severe bruising on her right thigh. Could she walk? She stirred one leg and then the other. "I can lead you away from here."

"And then what?" Joey whispered. "I'm dying, Jenny. And so are you. I guess you'll have to stay with me."

Jenny shivered. Joey didn't lie, but he certainly got things wrong. How to tell him that she had won by surviving the crash, and he had lost? He wouldn't like that. She would have to tell him gently. Wake him up to the truth, and then to a return to life.

"This is just a dream in the ghost world," she said. "I survived the real crash."

"Did you?" His voice sounded weaker, but amusement was clear in his tone.

"After a while, I was so sad that you died that I went to live with Frances."

"Her."

"I met …" She didn't look up, but her mind's eye saw Moira walking across the water. "I met some new friends."

"Is that what you remember? Living with Frances, finding new friends?" He turned his head slightly and his gaze met hers. "Jenny, Jenny, don't you understand yet?"

She thought she did understand, with heartbreaking clarity. She and Joey were only reliving the accident, and so far she had changed nothing. If she didn't get him out of this car, she was certain that he would die again. And — chilling thought — again. What had he said? *Once, or an infinite number of times.* She moved her legs, and the pain stopped. If she could get the car door open, she felt confident that she could walk away. But would he follow? He never followed, always led.

She played what she believed to be her strongest card. "If you don't come with me, I'll have to say goodbye forever. I'll have to let you go. And that means you'll stay a ghost forever, and go wherever ghosts go, without me. But here is the good news. I've dreamed about the crash. I've dreamed of you dying. My nightmares were just bad memories. But today, in this car, I can feel the heat from the engine. And I smell gasoline, and" — she nearly said *your blood*—"everything is all far too real to be a dream. And if I'm not dreaming, then there is still hope."

"It depends on what you hope for, Jenny."

"I'm going to have to crawl over you to open the driver's door and pull you out of here. Brace yourself. It will probably hurt."

"Jenny, don't worry." A trickle of blood ran down his temple past his ear. "You'll never have to say goodbye."

She struggled up to kneel on the seat. "Because you'll come with me?"

"No. Because we're both dead. Or maybe we're dying."

He never blinked, or maybe she'd missed it when she'd blinked herself.

"Don't tell lies, Joey. The one thing about you is that you never lie."

"It's true. You're the liar. And I sincerely appreciate all the lies you told for my benefit. Now sit back down."

She sat back in the car seat and stared at him. She began to understand what he was driving at. She hated it. She hated it like she hated the blood in his hair and the way his hand lay awkwardly, palm up, on his lap.

"Jenny, you're dying right now. It's still March in reality, and we're in the Zed."

"It's July, and I'm right about this." In this mood, he'd never agree to follow her. She'd have to strongarm him. The pain she'd been feeling had rolled back, as if her own injuries had lessened magically as soon as she realized she could take him out of here. He would be too heavy in the real world. But this was not the real world. Here, one walked on water and flew through the air. Therefore, if she took his hand, she might succeed in dragging him after her.

She leaned towards him, closed her eyes, and kissed him. "Just believe me, Joey. I went to the hospital and got better. And now I've come back for you."

"I'm afraid you've got it all wrong, Jenny," he murmured. "I think I died a moment or two before you did, maybe shortly after impact. Isn't that just like me, to go first? Isn't that the way we do things?"

"You mean I followed you? Not that time. Not when you died."

"But you will."

"I won't. I remember everything. The police found you, and they bent over you, and they said——"

"I know what they would say, Jenny."

"They looked at you and said, 'Poor kid.'" In the policeman's mouth, the phrase had sounded sympathetic, but now it went a long way towards killing hope. She hurried on. "I survived, Joey, and then I had to live my life without you."

"Maybe that's what it feels like to you. But you know what they say about the last moment of life? It goes incredibly slowly. You see your life before you die. I see my past. You see your future, I guess. The one you might have had."

At last she let herself understand what he was trying to tell her.

He said, "This moment is all there is. You are still in the car, waiting, hoping for the police, the ambulance, to come."

She leaned away from him against the passenger door. "Are you saying that I imagined or dreamed it——the island, Frances, Malcolm, and Adrian? That I'm still in the car? Are you saying that it's still the night you died?"

"We're dying. Both of us, in the crash together. Right now. Yes."

"No." How could she live several months in a moment? How could she feel all those individual breaths breathed in and out over that much time? Two months of rising morning after morning from sleep, and lying down again at the end of each day.

She said, "Nobody could imagine the details of every conversation, of mourning you in grief counselling sessions, of eating all those meals ..."

"But you don't eat, do you? Everybody tells you so."

Jenny must have eaten. Rachel said she didn't, but she must have. She couldn't remember doing so, but no one could live without eating.

Without warning, her strength failed her and she fell sideways in her seat, landing on her shoulder. When she struggled to sit up again, she only succeeded in turning sideways, and her bloody arm brushed the door. She was more badly hurt than she'd believed. Where were the police? She was sure they ought to be here by now.

Was that a car engine cutting out? Her heart beat faster. "Someone's coming."

"The cops. They'll find us dead."

"They'll help."

"Help? They'll haul me from the car. Then they'll haul you out." *Poor kid.*

Or would the police officer say *poor kids?*

She tried to rise up to climb over Joey, but the pain returned and pinned her to the seat. She pictured Malcolm and remembered how he'd kissed her. She recalled Frances's rock-hard kindness to her, and children up to their knees in the ocean under a hot summer sky. She had not made these people up. No one had the brains to dream up that much detail.

But Joey said she was dead. Or dying. And Joey loved her. He'd help her if he could. He'd said so. He'd always said so.

Joey never lied. Certainly not to her.

The pain in her arm and leg deepened.

At another, sharper noise outside the car, she looked up. She saw the moonlit curve of a girl's face through the window above her.

Was it Rachel? Had Rachel somehow come to help?

Her thoughts spun so that she had to struggle to count back the months to the crash. If this really was still March, and she and Joey were dying in her Zed, then what they needed was help: immediate, swift, and wholehearted. And help was here, although she didn't know how her sister had found the wreck. Had she told Rachel where they were going? No.

Then it couldn't be Rachel.

Unless she'd followed them. Rachel always tried to follow them. Never was there such a devoted sister. "We're in here, damn you."

Rachel would save her. Rachel would save them both.

The figure drew closer. Not Rachel. Instead, Moira stepped out from behind the angled telephone pole and into plain view.

Chapter 25

When Moira was little, in her attic bedroom in the house on Dunbar Street, her grandmother used to hold her in her arms and sing a little ditty, a song that Moira vowed she'd sing to her own children someday.

Where did you come from, Moira dear?

Out of the everywhere, into the here.

Moira's grandmother had certainly got that right. Moira advanced out of the darkness, out of the everywhere, into … *here.* She studied the yellow car with interest. It was smashed to blazes against a telephone pole.

So this was where Jenny had got to.

Setting her fists on her hips, Moira scanned the broken windshield of the car, taking in the smashed and crooked hood. It was positively hugging that telephone pole. They'd hit it at a high speed, if she was any judge. She shook her head. For goodness sake.

Searching and searching for Philip and Jenny, and now *this*.

"Look at this set-up, will you?" She peered inside through the passenger window. Jenny's eyes were shut like those of a fairy-tale princess. Moira very much doubted that she would want Prince Charming to see her lying there with her shorts bunched around her thighs like that.

Moira bent to look deeper inside the yellow car. There in the driver's seat sat a blond fellow, staring at her out of his near eye. She remembered him. He wore his shirt untucked. A lovely dancer, but fresh as today's fish.

Moira was impressed by the whole bloody spectacle. What a car crash, what a scene.

To think the blond fellow had it in him.

He lifted his eyebrow to her. She tried the passenger door, but it wouldn't budge. She walked briskly around the car and tried the driver's door, which opened like sesame. There was blood in his hair, on the seat, and on the blanket stuffed down behind Jenny. God, the car stank. And what was that wailing noise? Police, she supposed. She poked the fellow with her index finger. "Got a name, fresh boy?"

He raised his hand from his lap. "Joey ..."

"That's right. I remember now." She poked him again, and he made a short, sharp noise. "Joe. I like that. Just an average Joe, except you've got a lot of blood on you."

"Help us?" the average Joe asked. "At least, help Jenny."

"I shouldn't lift a finger." Moira snorted. "Do you know what she did? She ran out on me."

"*I* know. Doesn't matter now."

Joe opened one eye and sent her a look to break a girl's heart. She was a sucker for a beseeching gaze like his, but at least she knew when she was a sucker, unlike others she could name.

"All right, I'll play." Moira ran around to the passenger side, took hold of Jenny's door, and heaved with everything she had. It groaned open at last and she leaned inside. What a gory pair these two made. "Oh," she murmured, playing it up. "Oh, how *sad*."

The average Joe nodded at her and then closed his eyes again. Or were they quite closed? She thought he was watching her through the slits. She certainly hoped he was, at any rate. This show was for him, after all.

"Young lovers—Jenny and her Joe. You loved each other so much you had to die together, like Romeo and Juliet."

Moira stood back and gazed at her friend Jenny. She wondered again, and with increased irritation, how the girl had gotten so pretty. Still, Moira supposed it wasn't entirely Jenny's fault. She reached down and pulled a lock of hair, damp and brown, off her friend's forehead. Jenny's dark lashes lay against her white cheek. This was a sight to invoke pity in the most pitiless observer. There was no way to clean up her fellow, though.

"Do you have to bleed like that, Joe?" There was a flap of cloth hanging loose from the roof of the car. She ripped it free and covered a bloody place in his shoulder.

"Thank you," he said softly.

She smothered a laugh. He was sweet for a masher. "Anytime. Okay, now. What's next?" A moment's thought brought the answer. "*I* know."

There was that old blanket on the ledge behind the car seats. She reached over Jenny and tugged that out first. Stars in a dark sky looked down on her as she spread the blanket on the blacktop next to the car, and across the street a cat leaped on a fence to watch.

Moira returned to the passenger door and, with a mighty effort, wrenched it open. She took hold of Jenny's arm and pulled.

The girl's eyes opened wide, and Moira heard Joe hiss, "No! Don't move her."

"You just lie there and look pretty, Joe." Moira pulled harder. Jenny had the scene all wrong. First of all, only cheap girls wore cut-off shorts, like maybe to pick peaches or strawberries. Jenny should have worn a skirt. For the rest, it was a question of getting Jenny's centre of gravity off the seat, and then she'd fall the rest of the way. "I know what I'm doing."

Joe said, "For god's sake, be careful. She has internal injuries."

"Stop worrying. I've got the whole thing under control. Come on, Jenny."

Jenny was heavier than you'd think. Moira dragged the girl out legs first so that first one foot and then the other foot thumped out of the car. Moira pulled her clear of the car door and arranged her legs and feet to lie side by side like produce in a market stall. She straightened Jenny's shorts. She fanned out the brown hair. Jenny was wearing it far too long, even longer than Moira wore hers. She shook her head. "Who do you think you are with that hair? A movie star?"

The lashes on the pale cheeks fluttered. Moira sat back on her heels and waited.

"Can you look?" Jenny whispered. "I think I'm bleeding from my arm."

"Most of the blood's in the car." Moira gave her cheek a sharp pat. "I give you a hard time, but I must say you look enchanting. Fold your hands on your breast, now."

"I can't move."

That Jenny, she was always such a liar. Not a problem if you knew about her falsehoods, of course. Jenny was like a clock that was always nineteen minutes fast, and no problem if you could do the arithmetic. "Sure you can move. Do I have to do everything myself?"

Jenny moved one hand, then the other, onto her breast.

"See, was that so hard?"

Jenny shook her head, and as she did so, a tear ran out of the side of her left eye. Moira liked the effect. She decided not to wipe it away.

Joe's mouth opened, and it was too red inside, but that was the scene. He said, "Damn you to hell, Moira. You shouldn't have moved her. Don't you know better than to move a body?"

Moira rose to her feet. "You're spoiling the whole scene."

"The cops are going to come," he said. "They'll arrest you for manslaughter."

"I don't like your tone." She was bored with the play-acting. She'd been a good sport, but enough was sufficient. "Come on, Jenny. Let's go."

Jenny said, "*Poor kid.* That's what the cops said. *Poor kid.*"

"*Poor . . . ?*" Moira snorted. "Poor *sap*, more like. You, that is. Come on, Jenny, get up." She nudged her friend with her toe. "Don't you know when this fellow is pulling your chain?"

"I'm dead. Or at least I'm dying." Jenny closed her pretty eyes.

"I thought it was July, and it's March. That's why I see him and I see you. Because I'm dead."

"Of course you're not dead. You'd *know* if you were dead," Moira said. "It's July, silly Jenny. You told me Joe's been dead since March. Can you really not tell when a fellow is shining you on?"

Moira took a step back to watch it sink in. Jenny raised herself, first on one elbow and then the other.

"Joey?" There was no answer from the car. Jenny got to her feet and leaned inside the open driver's door. "You told me I was dead, Joey. You told me I was dying. Right here, right now. You lied to me? Joey, you never lie."

At that, Moira bent down to get a better look at an actual male of the species who didn't lie.

How handsome he looked, even with bloody hair.

"You told me you saved me." Jenny reached out a hand, and Moira bet herself that Joe was going to find himself slapped, and rightly slapped at that. But before Jenny could touch him, he opened his mouth just a little. Just a little, but wide enough to let a sentence fall from between his lips, one word after the next, like a line of rolling pearls.

"Oh, Jenny," he said, "how could I know you all my life and never learn to tell a lie?"

Moira pulled Jenny away from the car. She pulled plenty hard, because there was nothing wrong with Jenny now.

Jenny shook Moira off and turned back towards Joey. The look in her eye was so bitter that Moira stood back, the better to see the show play out.

Jenny said, "You don't love me, Joey. I don't ever want to see you again. You are ..."

Moira could wait no longer. "Say it. Hurry up."

"Joey, you are dead to me," Jenny said.

"I couldn't have put it better myself," Moira said. She took hold of Jenny and led her away, out of the here and back to the everywhere. There would be danger ahead, but Moira was fine with danger as long as she had a friend along. As long as she had Jenny, the two of them could change anything. Dare anything.

Double dare.

AMBIENCE

Jason P Burnham

Jason P Burnham loves to spend time with his wife, children, and dog. His work has previously appeared in Mixtape: 1986, Nature: Futures, *and* Strange Horizons, *among others. Find him on Twitter at @AndGalen.*

$\mathcal{A}$MBIENCE

I was ECSTATIC when the apocalypse hit.

If I had paid attention to the news before it stopped broad-casting, I probably could have figured out what turns people into zombies, but it just doesn't interest me.

What *does* interest me? Zombie-vacated homes. It's like I'm the star in my very own apocalyptic *Best Crib in Town*. *The judges have spoken. Mx Braineater, you have the Best Crib in Zombie Town!*

The only things hampering my unbridled domicile debauchery are the vexatious vagabonds that want my grey matter for a snack. Today, just two stiffs stand in my way of the amazing mansion down the road.

"Back off!" I whisper-shout. Sometimes it works.

Grrrrhhhh.

What a boring thing to say for the entirety of an un-life. I run into the nearest house, a total design disaster.

"Gross!" *Another* Yoda-dressed-as-Santa knickknack. That's eight this week! Don't people tire of having the same garbage as everyone else?

Grrrrhhhh, comes the zombies' call from behind.

Right, weapons. I hated weapons pre-apocalypse, and guns

have become even *more* distasteful now because they summon the hordes.

"UGH!" I should stop being surprised at how prominently displayed the guns are in some houses. This one has a rifle *and* a machete under a buck's taxidermied head. A bit on the nose.

One shambler has fallen in the foyer onto the god-awful faux-tiger rug. The zombie's spilling offal can only improve the ambience.

I pick up the machete. *Zing*—off with their heads. I wipe sticky black residue onto the orange-and-black-striped fake. On the bright side, this travesty of a house is going to make that mansion at the end of the road seem even more spectacular.

This ... this may well be the crown jewel of Vacant House Voyeurism. If television still existed, that's what I would call my show.

It's like Fallingwater by Frank Lloyd Wright, but with *my* quirks. Maybe the former owner and I would have been kindred spirits.

Like Wright's most famous house, a river runs through it. *Beautiful*. Not only that, but it is utilitarian. *Be still, my heart!* And my loins if it turns out the owner didn't convert—though I have my doubts with that wide-open front door.

A purification system runs into the basement and pumps clean, fresh water through the house. And! There are still-functioning solar panels on the roof. Walking through the living area, I see all the lights are on, seemingly hydroelectrically powered. A girl could get used to this.

Pragmatism aside, this is a delectable dwelling. A stone fireplace. A reading nook under the staircase. A delightfully claustrophobic half-bath on the top floor, with a creek overlook. The master bedroom's padded reading area faces west so you can read *and* watch the sunset. A four-story interior waterfall cascades alongside a spiral stone staircase. If there ever was an idyllic house, I'm standing in it.

Shoes shuffle below, and my grip on the machete tightens. Time to reprise my role as the Geomancy Guillotine. This house is too amazing *not* to clear out; I may never leave.

I creep to the balcony to see if this one can climb stairs.

"Hey! What are you doing in my house?" shouts a woman.

I shrink away from the balustrade, unsure what to say. My silence gets me a warning shot.

"Hey, watch it!" I yell.

"Sorry. Thought you might be a …"

"Zombies don't talk," I respond.

"You didn't answer my question," says the woman.

My palms sweat, anticipating a meeting with the curator of this palace. "Is this really your house?"

"Yes, and I intend to keep it that way. I would appreciate it if you would *get out*."

I ignore the request to leave. "It's remarkable," I say.

"What?"

She wasn't expecting me to say *that*. I move carefully to the edge—no bullets this time. "I love your home. It is simultaneously exquisite and utilitarian and …"

The owner is gorgeous, and I unwittingly float down the spiral staircase toward her.

"That's nice of you to say, but don't get too close," she says, backing away, gun raised.

"Hmm?" I'm lost in her resplendent brown eyes. Thick auburn hair tumbles to her waist, caressing lustrous ochre skin.

"You complimented my house?" Her eyes twitch in confusion.

Who does she remind me of? Or … *what?* I stammer out a response. "Y-y-you designed this house in your own image. The goddess designed Valhalla in a mirror."

She blushes and lowers her gun.

"Did you …" My heart races, hesitant to reveal my guilty pleasure. "Did you ever watch *Best Crib in Town?*"

She waves her hand and says in a deep dramatic voice, "The judges have spoken …"

I smile, a happy shiver running down my spine. I think this apocalypse is going to work out just fine.

CAN-ON-A-STRING

Alex Kitt

Alex Kitt (he/him) is a writer and poet born in Red Deer, Alberta. He holds a BFA in Creative Writing from the University of British Columbia. His poem 'complicated grief' appears in Pulp Literature *Issue 34*, and he has recent work in White Wall Review. *He currently resides in Montréal.*

Can-on-a-String

We moved back to our old town, my sister Lynn and I, and shoved our lives between the bed stands, boxes, and dust of Uncle's home. That first week, I drew faces in the dust and sometimes I'd laugh at what I came up with, or I'd laugh at the way one drawing might look up at me. Laughter was good, but now I see how all those faces were *me* spread out, my laughter in the attic and my sorrow next to the washer/dryer.

Two months passed before anything began to change. Two more months of dust, layering and layering. Lynn would use the lint roller on her head before she left for work.

Dear Ms Trebbo,

I am writing to you for the Exploration Geologist position at Kingfinn Metals Corp. I believe that I may be a great fit for the position because I am highly motivated to gain experience in exploration field geology as a newly registered geologist-in-training. I have recently completed my Bachelor of Science degree, majoring in Earth and Atmospheric Sciences at the University of Alberta, and I am keen to integrate myself into a career path that I am truly passionate about.

The fact is that at *this* moment — if someone would hire me — I could be in a gold mine or on the side of a glacier. In an interview, one company asked if I knew how to shoot a rifle in case of bears. I could be a bear-rifle person on the side of a mountain. But I'm not.

I could be with the friends I made in uni. The ones who rushed from class to class, complaining about their grogginess, the weather, petty things — which are the best things in life to complain about. These complaints mean their lives are bright, their futures are unafflicted and open. And I could be with them, moving forward. But I'm not.

I'm home.

Uncle got dementia. It was only Lynn and me. So we came home.

For good reason too, I thought. I hoped that upon seeing Uncle, or an old friend, or the objects or streets of my childhood, or even upon hearing some turn of phrase from Lynn I'd forgotten, maybe I'd feel something good. But Uncle is less of himself; he's turned into a doddering old man — a twisted relay. My hometown friends look weather-beaten, the way a child's toy does if it's abandoned outside. And Uncle's house is just a graveyard. He had taken in most of our parents' things after their death — the objects all spirits that spiral me back into myself, or into the other people I used to be, a thousand times over.

I want to say we've come full circle. I got my old job back at Starbucks. Lynn and I are forced to talk to each other again. But maybe it's not so much a full circle as it is a gross distortion of the past. When I finally found Fifo — the dog we had bought Uncle a few years before — he was long dead, mixed in with the mountain of trash in the backyard. It seemed to confirm things. Our past is not behind us, but a forest of years that surrounds us, its wind blowing through us. Hour after moth-eaten hour, I work and clean to get us out.

I try to tell Lynn about this, but I can tell she's thinking about other things.

I try because I worry.

And I worry because I think she's stealing again.

I've been cleaning up Uncle's yard to get the house in order so we can sell it. But bikes, bags full of bottles, and small things, like lawn gnomes, have been accumulating. Lynn shoplifted as a kid. So did I. But she's almost twenty-five. She should know better.

And I worry because of other things, too. I went with her to the aggression workshop that, I thought, her work was forcing her to attend. But I wouldn't ask because I knew she wouldn't tell.

She has become an unfamiliar person, but with the same sort of life-in-reverse as me. I want her to know that she needs to run. That we need to run.

The aggression workshop was on a Tuesday evening in the community college's art studio. Everything in the room was in muted shades of brown, with sections of the walls and various tables and stools accosted by paint splatter. There was one large window above the one counter, which contained four sinks. Two of them had tape Xing out their basins, and 'out of order' was scrawled in loopy letters on signs above. The college catered to trades and sciences, so the fine-arts wing was old and in need of renovations. But the studio seemed to have it the worst. After we moved some easels out of the way and found some chairs, it didn't take long for me to figure out I was in a room with ex-cons and court-mandated workers eager to prove it was 'all a misunderstanding'.

There were ten of us, excluding the instructor, Caroline Hay—"Hey, hey, I'm Caroline Hay!"—who did her best to open the conversation. No one seemed to give a shit. Caroline looked like every second yoga mom who walked into Starbucks, smelling of Zen and placing their order in a tone that clearly meant 'fuck off'. Her hair was tied so tightly in a ponytail she couldn't have wrinkled her forehead if she tried. I wanted a definitive reason to make her a villain, but despite everything, you could tell she was just a good person trying her best.

Pasha, from my old neighbourhood, was there. And Freedom, Tina, Lane. Sitting respectfully, voices low, only moving to look up sharply as the door opened and shut behind yet another sad soul. Everyone seemed to be seated as far back within themselves as possible.

My shoelaces were untied. Both of them. I could tie them both. Or I could tie one or the other. I thought about these little variations that would maybe end up changing my life.

Caroline had everyone introduce themselves and make a small speech about what they hoped to learn in the workshop. When it came to me, I gave a fake name and didn't add much else.

Caroline brought out some nails, hammers, aluminum cans, Scotch tape, and string. She wanted us to do an anonymous phone call exercise to break down 'our barriers'.

The cans popped, and no one said a word. From across the room, I watched Lynn lift her hammer, the light landing deep in the purple moons beneath her eyes. She squinted, and for a moment she looked much older. Somehow, I remembered an old dream in which my roommate was eating my can of beans and I did nothing to stop him. That was in my first year of university. Lynn never came to visit; we never called each other.

Sometimes I saw her on social media, in the background of one of her friend's photos, wearing the same green cardigan she wore almost everywhere, the one she was wearing now. The front pockets sank with the weight of lip balm, car keys, wallet, and whatever else. She jingled when she walked.

There was a guy still wearing his suit jacket, like he might leave at any moment. Tyler. He was clutching his hand to his chest. He must have missed the nail and smashed his hand, or mishandled the nail. I didn't see any blood. He made no noise, but it was the commotion with the man he'd been partnered with that caught my attention. His partner—this big guy—grabbed him by the shoulder and was trying to pull him to the paint-smattered sinks. Tyler kept saying "I'm fine. I'm fine. I'm fine." The big man dragged him over to the sink, pulled a flask from his pocket, and poured a splash of rum onto Tyler's hand, saying "tetanus, tetanus," while someone else shouted objections to his reasoning. It was then that Tyler finally raised his voice and said, "For fuck's sake!" Everyone stared. No one moved. Tyler looked at everyone looking at him. And in the silence, I think everyone thought the same thing. Everyone realized where we were, and that we were not who we thought we were, or who we wanted to be, but rather that we were much closer to the *less* we were afraid of.

> *As a recent graduate, I have gained many practical skills throughout my degree. I believe my core-logging skills make me a strong candidate since I excelled in several courses with labs that focused on creating dozens of reports in which I described and interpreted core.*

Things kept showing up in Uncle's backyard. The other day, our neighbour called out to me while I was working in the backyard. "You must be a collector!" he said, with obvious scepticism. So I covered up the gnomes, bikes, camp stoves, and fancy deck chairs with a tarp. I tried to stay awake when Lynn went on her drives, but I always fell asleep before she got home. Every morning there was more — more maroon ten-speeds, more lawn gnomes, more lawn chairs, more little George Foreman grills. Every morning I stood with my coffee and looked at what Lynn had collected.

We were all blindfolded except for Caroline, who had begun to guide people across the room to random stools and hand them each a can connected with string to another one. Someone nearby was knocking their can against something, maybe a ring on their finger. The thump-thump-thump lifted the silence and filled the room with a sense of premonition. It was an ambivalent gesture, but the longer we all spent with it, the more it seemed Caroline was a medium to a strange act we were all about to commit. I flinched when I felt her hand on my shoulder; I must have been the last one to be moved. She directed me across the room. We did what felt like two laps before she sat me down in what I thought was the seat I started in. She gave me an aluminum can. I could hear rain begin to tap lightly against the windows.

"Okay," Caroline began, and the can thumper ceased. "We are all now no longer who we were. We are formless. We do not contain ourselves. We are now vessels of voice."

Somebody scoffed.

"Feel free now to say whatever it is you feel you need to say. Aggression is simply a vile opposite of what we feel we cannot say. Try to find the opposite of your past voice. Dig within yourself to find more of what you are."

I heard Tyler's voice loud in his can across the room: "I am a fish." Everyone laughed. But then the room began to echo, murmurs of vibrato speech sounds unidentifiable in their number.

I felt the string on the end of my can grow tight. I held it up to my ear and heard a little voice: "… I grew up like that. They were really emotional. But they would not deal with their feelings." I had missed the beginning. I moved the can toward my mouth to say this but stopped. I put the can back to my ear. "She has a tendency to attack. And she doesn't understand how the things that she does affect other people, and she doesn't care. She would be like, 'Well, it's your problem. Why are you mad at me?' So I've had to kind of remove her from my life, and that was good for me. But now she is dying, and she is extra not-nice to me. And it's so bad for me, but I am now with her all over again, and I don't want that—" I took the can from my ear. It felt good to hold my voice in my hand. It felt *really* good, and I thought I might laugh, until someone flicked my forehead.

"You haven't opened up yet," Caroline said. She smelled like the popcorn stand in the mall.

The good feeling went away, and my throat closed up. There was a tug at the string.

"You're the only one who didn't reserve a spot. You need to at least say something," Caroline said. The popcorn essence wafted over me. "Open up."

I turned away from her, but I was looking, still, at nothing.

A cliff of silence loomed, and I knew she had gone. I felt another tug at the can. I held it up to my mouth. "I think you should give up on her," I said.

Another small tug on the can. I switched it to my ear. "Why? She's one of the only ones there."

"Is that important?" I felt uncomfortable now with Caroline watching me. I tugged on my nose; it was my uncle's nervous tick. I had never done this before. It made me think about his arched eyebrows, his permanent squint, his stubby old nose. When I was a child, I would tug on his nose and he would honk. I wondered what he might do now, or if he'd even remember.

Another tug at the can.

"I don't think you know what you're talking about," the voice said.

Lately, when Lynn got off work, she crashed onto the couch and drank some vodka sodas while watching TV with Uncle. After he passed out for the night, she went back out, getting in her little blue Toyota and driving off. Once, I chased her on my bike. I wanted to catch her in the act. I wanted to scream at her, to scream her name and catch her amidst her life, caught like a deer in headlights. I couldn't keep up with her, though. At some intersections I'd get near, but I needed to catch her in the act. She pulled a U-turn, and I rode my bike right into a hedge for cover. If she caught me chasing her for answers, well …

Popcorn Caroline was hovering again. She wanted me to say something into the can. What was I supposed to say? "My parents are dead." What would that help? They are dead. That night when I was looking for Lynn, I wondered if I had processed anything. If Lynn had processed anything. I pedalled through the streets and moved through my thoughts without ever arriving anywhere. On my bike, feeling the sweat-fractured closeness to the world, I thought about all these things, like how night doesn't fall so hard in the shadows. I could convince myself I was profound. I saw how if I fully abandoned myself to memory and speculation and searching, I could convince myself of anything. How if I was so deep inside myself, I didn't really exist outside myself. So I kept scanning the streets, trying to hold on to reality, and searching for Lynn, until a good number of windows were lit up and dawn was snuffing out streetlights and I realized I would have only two hours of sleep before work, before it all began again.

Caroline was still waiting for me to say something. I held the can to my mouth. "I'm going to get a good job, meet someone good, and leave this place. For good."

I have an extensive background in mineral identification, where my knowledge has been tested in field settings.

"I don't have any family. I know nobody," I said. It didn't feel like a lie.

It was raining hard against the window by the time Caroline switched us all again. I hoped I'd be matched with Lynn, but I also just wanted to go home. Even if I asked her about her night drives, would Lynn tell the truth? Before our parent's death I was already far from her. The sooner I got home tonight, the sooner I could apply for more jobs in cities better than this one. I heard the shuffling of feet. Whoever had been softly tapping their aluminum can kept on with it as we were shifted around the room in our blindfolded darkness. Over the next half hour, with the can to my ear, I heard story after story.

"It was one of the biggest errors in my life. And I've been carrying it around all my life."

"Do you know how many people are idiots?"

"For me, they were the closest person in my life, and they just went away."

"I knew that I would feel guilty for a long time. I just didn't think it would be so heavy … I let him get run over by a tractor."

None of these voices were my sister's. Some might have been the people I knew back in high school. Each voice pulled me down and down into the deepest parts of myself. Are you anyone if you're in relation to no one at all?

I am also competent using technology, having utilized ArcGIS for differentiating types of data and creating maps and having worked with geoSCOUT for researching oil and gas play for a term project.

When Caroline instructed us to take our blindfolds off, all the colours that were splattered about the room poured into my eyes like paint swirling into water. It had stopped raining. Caroline said something about what it meant to her that we all did such a good job letting out our emotions. Then everyone clapped for her, and she did a little curtsy. Everyone began to pull apart all the cans and tape and string, and then we discarded them in the blue bin by the door. Caroline approached me and said, "You should think about coming to the next one. The first Tuesday of every month!"

Lynn came up to me with a bit of a smile. "You ready, Freddy?"

"Spaghetti!" Caroline joked for me. "Hope to see you again?"

Lynn replied, "I think you will. I didn't know what to expect."

We exited the college and walked up the sidewalk to the gravel parking lot. I couldn't remember where Lynn had parked, so I let her lead. The air had been washed clean by the rain. The clouds had moved off, and the sun was low. It shone through a row of spruce trees swaying in what was left of the wind. Lynn's car was cool, and we sat for a moment, staring out at the high-way. Lynn's breath oscillated, fast then slow, condensing on the driver-side window.

"Well. What did you think?" she asked. The way Lynn sat so low in her seat behind the wheel reminded me of a grandma.

"I don't know. What did you think?"

She sighed, and her breath swelled on the window. "I thought it was good."

"Yeah?"

"Yeah. I'm glad I signed myself up."

This came as a bit of a shock. She wasn't mandated by her work to go. We watched the other vehicles pull out of the lot one by one. Someone in a lifted truck drove straight across the sports field, around the tall fence, up the shoulder, and onto the highway. I thought it must have been the big man with the flask.

"How often do you think about Mom and Dad?" Lynn asked. She turned away from the window to face me but then turned back.

"I don't know." I picked at the lint on my pants. "Maybe—maybe half a second every day? But then some days, at least half an hour."

"Right." We watched the rest of the workshoppers stub out their cigarettes and drive off, or duck into cars picking them up at the curb. When the last car disappeared around the corner, Lynn started the Toyota. Dash lights and A/C pulled us back from wherever we each had gone. This was my chance to ask her if she was the one stealing all the stuff that kept showing up in the yard.

"How has the job search been going?" she asked.

I have worked on and presented field projects where outcrops were observed and catalogued with base maps, lithologs, and cross sections.

"Meh." I fluttered my hand. "What did you talk about? Through the can. What did you say?"

After a few seconds, she answered, "I talked about Uncle mostly." She laughed. "About his smell. How gross that living room smells now that he's been parked in it." I remembered the mould I had cleaned out of the fridge, and the smell of the dog carcass as I shovelled it into a heavy-duty garbage bag. "Honestly, I talked about everything."

"Everything? What's everything?"

She made a broad gesture. "Like. All of it."

"Lynn. C'mon."

"Well. You know, I've been sorting out a home to get Uncle into. That's been hard." She put the Toyota into reverse and then put it back into park. "You know what he said to me the other day?"

"Hm?"

"He said, 'I haven't had this much family around since I was a boy sharing a room with your father.'" Lynn shook her head. She reversed, then drove out of the lot. She flicked the broken blinker that chose either to work double-time or not to work at all. "I talked about you a bit. Mostly about Uncle, though. Nothing about Mom or Dad — but, well, I guess a bit. They show up everywhere and in everything it seems."

Looking way out west, you could see the storm we must've just caught the edge of. Lightning lit the sky, but it was too far off to hear thunder. I didn't say anything back to Lynn.

"I talked about this thing." She pulled off the Highway 1 exit early. "Do you remember, when we were little, how I always used to get so angry with you? And Uncle, even, and just start screaming?" We drove slowly through a suburb in the general direction of our own suburb, in the fold where city met farmland. Streetlights held moths and mosquitoes like jars. A guy was walking his dachshund.

"Here," Lynn said, and rolled down her window. "I'm gonna kill your dog!" she yelled at the dog walker. Then she punched the gas and sped off around the corner.

"What the fuck? Dude!" I yelled.

Lynn kind of smiled, but I could tell it was something else.

"What? Tell me!" I would have kept saying "what" if Lynn hadn't spoken.

"That's it. That's what I meant. About how I deal with our parents—sort of. I don't know. I used to do it when I was drunk in university, driving around with friends for a laugh. But now I—don't look at me like that!"

"Do you have a problem? Like! Like—"

"I do. Don't you? Don't you have a problem?"

For some reason I pictured Fifo, our half-assed attempt at giving Uncle some companionship, before I shovelled him into the bag. On her night drives, Lynn wasn't stealing bikes and stuff. She was screaming at people, disposing of her anger. My ears were on fire, and my heart was racing. "Do you know where all the stuff in the yard is coming from?" I asked.

Lynn smiled big. "Uncle."

"What?" We were near our neighbourhood, and Lynn turned left.

"Yeah. Late at night. I usually try to track him down, but he's quick."

"Oh. Wow." Just like with everything, this felt like something else. "What home is Uncle gonna go in?" I asked.

"There's only one with a dementia ward."

I thought about how Uncle had reconfigured the living room so that he didn't have to go up to his bedroom anymore. He'd brought down his Smith-Corona typewriter and a bunch of boxes of old files from when he worked as a teacher. He was always sleeping during the day when I came home from my morning shifts at Starbucks. Asleep on the floor, surrounded by all those boxes, old student papers lying everywhere. Sleeping like the dead inside a coffin. When I woke him up to get him on the couch, I wondered if he actually was fully awake, fully aware of what was happening to him. He would put his hand on my shoulder as I helped him up, and even when I set him down on the couch he kept it there. He'd done the same when I was a kid. It was an old gesture—my dad had done it too. Whenever I got Uncle to lie down, his mind was somewhere else, yet his body was stuck—stuck in the movement of who he used to be.

Lynn stopped bobbing her head to the radio and looked back and forth between me and the road. "It'll be okay."

I didn't respond. We were on our street now. Someone was jogging on the sidewalk. I looked at Lynn with horror, wondering if she would scream again.

She looked at me with a smile I hadn't seen in years. With a raspy whisper-shout just loud enough for me to hear, she said, "Wherever you're runnin', you'll never get there."

OEUFS DANGEREUX

Pete Barnstrom

Pete Barnstrom is an award-winning screenwriter and filmmaker whose projects have played at theatres and film festivals all over the world. He's shot documentaries in Greenland for the National Science Foundation, made movies with the Blair Witch guys (not that one), and seen one of his films screened at the Smithsonian. You can find him on Twitter at @MistahPete and on Instagram at mistah.pete.

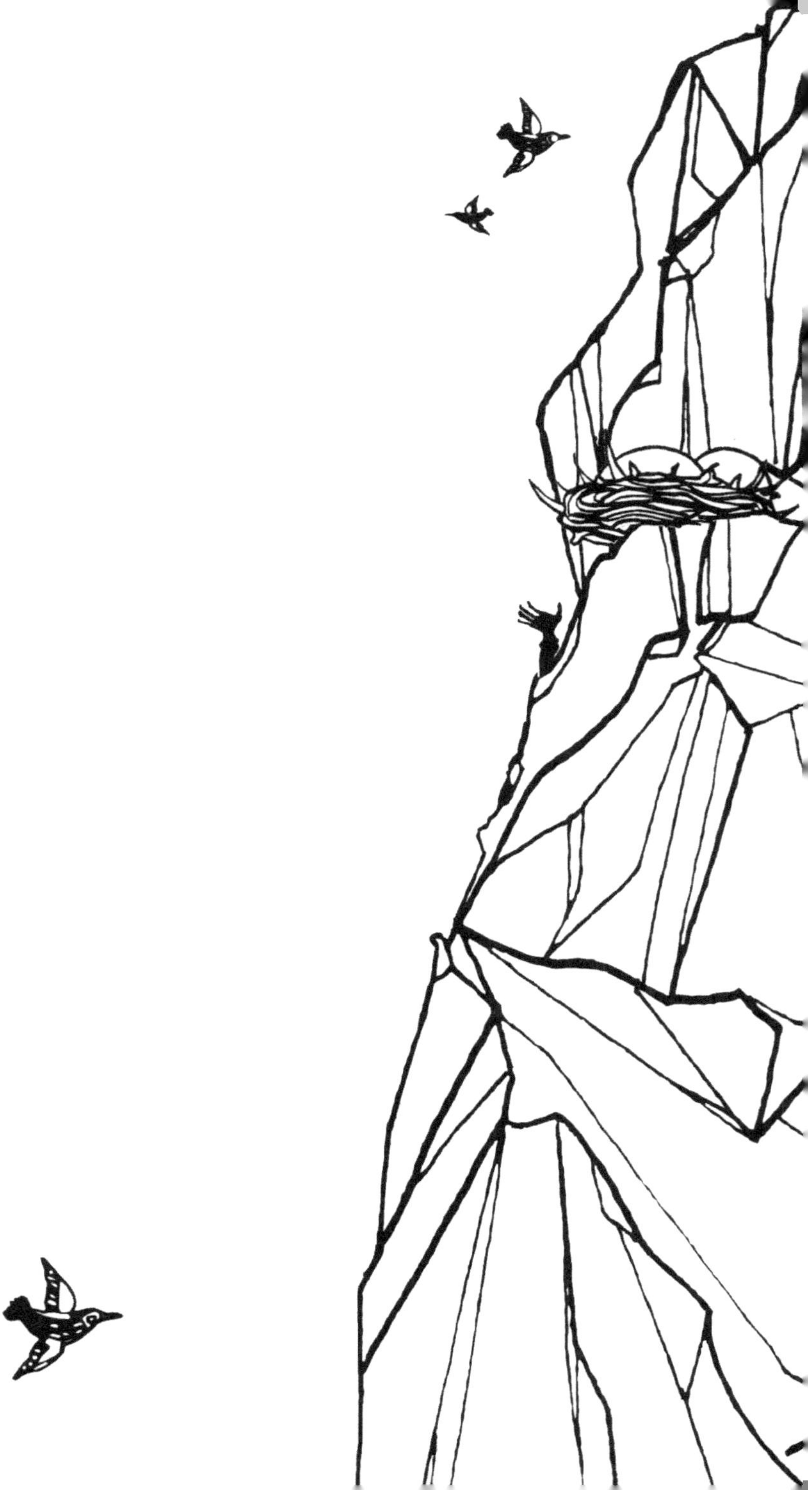

Oeufs Dangereux

The lines sang complaints against the rocks overhead. The rope through Henri's harness was tight, but he was well below its tensile strength. Henri paid the sounds no mind.

Neither did he worry about Poco, who was feeding out the rope from above. Henri outweighed Poco by at least twenty kilos, and a tumble down the walls of the rugged cliff into the primordial jungle below would be an end most unpleasant. But Poco's devotion was absolute. It was not the first time Henri had placed his life in Poco's hands, and he trusted it would not be the last.

No, what concerned Henri was the sky.

He cast glances over his impeccably tailored shoulder as he descended, looking for any indication of huge wings, razor talons as long as his arm, a shrieking maw seeking to rend him to so much tartare.

He saw none.

But below, he saw the nest perched on a large crag. And a clutch of eggs—he could count at least seven from his precarious position. Surely the mother would not begrudge him, say, three? Imagine the inconvenience of seven snapping snouts to feed. Four would be much more manageable.

Henri bounded off the wall before him, dropping with each bounce. Three, four, five, and now he was within a metre of the nest. Impatient, he landed amid the melon-sized eggs, barely keeping his balance. It would not do to crush one of the delicate beauties, no, not after all this effort.

Tugging a glove off between his teeth, he eyed the orbs with victorious avarice. Slowly, gently, he touched the surface of the eggs, one after another, running his hands across the smooth surfaces as he would the round haunch of a lover, or perhaps the rind of an especially smelly cheese.

Henri did not consider himself a spiritual man, not in the least, but he did believe with all of his corporeal being in a communion between himself and food. He could feel which of these were to go into his satchel, and which were to be left behind to gestate and grow and one day produce more eggs for him upon his return.

He made his selections. Not so delicate as he'd expected. Sturdy, these shells, more like ceramic tile than the chicken eggs he'd collected in his innocent youth. He wondered if he'd need special tools to crack them.

It was only once he'd placed three eggs, carefully wrapped, into his bag, that Henri heard the terrible scream.

He turned and saw, in the blue-sky distance, an ominous silhouette, leathern wings flapping, the huge beak open and calling its chilling cry. Coming at him.

Le ptérodactyle.

Henri tugged on the rope to alert faithful Poco to pull. The rope fell, the frayed end flapping past him, down the cliff far below.

This, he acknowledged, was cause for concern.

Poco, in the meantime, had problems of his own. Steadfast Poco, stout-hearted Poco, had been there, the rope looped around a tree and tethered to his own waist. He was not large, it was true, but Poco was a strong man, and there was nothing that could prevent him from returning Henri to safety.

Or so he believed, until he was introduced to the baby ankylosaurus.

Although Henri had brought him to this mysterious and secluded valley more than once, Poco did not know the name of the spiny beast. Others like it had been pointed out to him before, and he'd been assured that they were herbivores, and so harmless.

Words like 'harmless' do not mean the same to everyone. While this creature was smaller than others he'd seen, and so likely a juvenile, it was still nearly as large as the average cow, and quite imposing as far as Poco was concerned.

It was an ungainly thing, this young ankylosaur, and it seemed to want his attention. The animal approached without fear, nudging at him. Did it expect him to play with it? Feed it? Well, it was bound for disappointment, as Poco would not be swayed from his duties.

At first, Poco tried to ignore it. He swung a few half-hearted kicks at the animal, told it to shoo.

Soon, however, he remembered that where a child went, a mother was sure to follow. It would not do to have a protective mother dinosaur confronting him about her baby, no matter how many vegetables she might prefer to eat.

And so Poco found a rock and bounced it off the colossal baby's shell. This proved to be an error on his part.

He saw the club-tail swing at him just in time to jump, but still it caught the heels of his boots and sent him tumbling. Poco rolled away from the animal to avoid any trampling or tail pummellings.

There came a tugging at his torso, and Poco saw that the little dinosaur was pulling on the rope, evidently under the impression that it was an extension of Poco's body.

Poco pulled back, not one to allow any baby monster to get the best of him.

And then the rope broke, he and the ankylosaur fell in different directions, and Poco realized just what a mistake he'd made.

His intended means of escape being no longer available, Henri would have to climb. The treetops seemed tantalizingly close, and so he started down. The beast was no hummingbird, and he could only hope that the huge pterodactyl had his own challenges hovering and so would be unable to peck him off of the cliff.

He had underestimated the pterodactyl.

It swooped at him from left and right, the jagged edges of the enormous beak snapping at him, narrowly missing his head and back, and at one point very nearly mussing his carefully styled hair. Henri ducked and dropped and almost fell, his fingertips clutching at the juts and cracks.

He chanced a look down; the jungle canopy below seemed no closer. The way that giant bird-lizard dived at him, Henri had but one choice if he was to avoid becoming a meal himself.

The first branch broke his fall, but fortunately not his back. He grabbed at the second, and while his grip did not hold, it at least slowed his fall. He landed across the third, belly on thorny bark, arms and legs splayed on either side, then slid off, and his next stop was the mulch-dense ground of the jungle floor.

There, he allowed himself a moment of rest.

Things were quiet. No doubt the fauna was startled into silence by the sound of his falling and possibly the sounds that escaped his person in the process. He did not remember speaking any specific words, but it was not hard to imagine there had been some well-chosen oaths and bellows.

Then, as if a relay had been thrown, the sounds rose around him. He heard birds and insects, and other things he could not identify. Each sound, he suspected, represented something that might have an interest in tasting him.

Henri got to his feet. In order to stay on them, he required the support of the tree that had slowed his fall, but he was up. He smoothed his hair and moustache, being a gentleman of priorities, and then assessed his body. He considered the various pains and lacerations and possible fractures, and decided he'd cracked nothing of importance.

That's when he remembered the eggs.

The satchel. Where was the satchel? He looked around the ground where he'd landed and didn't see it.

He looked up.

It hung from a branch. Too high to reach.

The base of the tree was too immense for him to shake the bag loose. But the peculiar striation of the trunk allowed his feet to find purchase, and he started up toward his satchel. The idea of more climbing held little appeal for Henri, but he'd come this far and was not about to abandon his eggs up there. Assuming they were even still whole.

He'd just reached the satchel when he heard voices below. Voices? In this prehistoric forest?

The first was a guttural growl he might've mistaken for an animal had he not recognized the sounds as language. "He came down somewhere around here, milady, I'd swear to it."

"Your oath means nothing to me, you buffoon."

Now, that was a voice Henri recognized. Lady Fortescue, the unscrupulous British gourmand and cookbook plagiarist. Which made the other voice that of her menacing footman, Balmonde.

Henri froze in the branches. The satchel was within arm's reach, but he dared not move lest he attract their attention.

That fiendish Fortescue woman would stop at nothing to take any potable Henri could hunt down, simply on the assumption that if Henri wanted it, it must be delicious. As it happened, she was correct, if not always successful.

"If he did not in fact strike land here, milady" — Henri again heard the bestial snarl of the killer Balmonde — "then one can only assume —"

And the two of them looked up, and they saw Henri in the branches above, his unmoving arm extended toward the suspended satchel.

Lady Fortescue smiled her decadent smile. "Might as well bring it down here to me, Frenchie," she drawled. "I shall have it one way or another."

As if to illustrate the unspoken threat, Balmonde produced an evil-looking pistol from his waistcoat and directed it up at Henri, his meaty finger squeezed inside the trigger guard. There was no way he could miss, not from this distance.

Henri saw no escape.

Then, as he watched, the villains' faces went pale. Lady Fortescue dropped her lorgnette, and Balmonde squealed like a frightened child.

Henri turned his head up, saw the dark blur coming at him, and he did not hesitate. He sprang forward, caught the satchel in his arms, and swung off the tree to the ground near the cliff wall just as a baby ankylosaur plunged down onto Fortescue's and Balmonde's horrified heads.

As the dinosaur righted itself, having fallen spikes first onto the pair of rotters, Henri peered up the cliff and saw a pair of arms waving down at him.

Ah, resolute Poco. One could always count on him to kick a baby dinosaur off a cliff at just the right moment.

Ignoring the moans coming from the crater in front of him, Henri snapped a salute at Poco then flipped open the satchel and peered inside.

The eggs, all three of them, still intact.

He nodded. This would be a superb meal indeed.

The Chevalier smiled wide as Poco lifted the silver cover from the tray. Three perfect eggs, mostly yolk, each the size of a child's head. Liberally seasoned with mysterious herbs and mushrooms procured from exotic lands at immeasurable price.

"Magnifique," he murmured.

Hand on the shoulder of his brave Spanish sous chef, Henri beamed with satisfaction.

"You have outdone yourself," the Chevalier continued. "Never have I seen a dish so exquisite!"

"You are too kind." Henri nodded. Poco's smile stretched across his face.

The Chevalier lifted his knife and fork, ran each piece against the other as if to sharpen them. He was going to enjoy this meal.

Then he looked up at Henri. "Do you think," he asked, "I could have some tomato catsup?"

Henri smiled indulgently at the old Chevalier.

"*Non,*" he said.

ADRIFT OFF THE SHORE OF ALZHEIMER ISLAND

Cheryl Skory Suma

Cheryl Skory Suma's fiction, creative non-fiction, and poetry have appeared in US, UK, and Canadian publications, including Barren Magazine, Blank Spaces Magazine, Longridge Review, and Reckon Review (forthcoming), among others. Cheryl is a Pushcart Prize nominee, and her work has placed in more than thirty competitions, including Five South's 2021 Short Fiction Prize, Ruminate Magazine's 2021 Waking Flash Prose Prize, and Exposition Review's 2022 Flash 405 Escape Contest. Cheryl has an MHSc in Speech-Language Pathology and an HBSc in Psychology. Find her on twitter @cherylskorysuma. 'Adrift off the Shore of Alzheimer Island' was the runner-up in our 2022 Bumblebee Flash Fiction Contest.

Adrift off the Shore of Alzheimer Island

She stumbles, a newborn in the insidious haze. Her sunset on life's shore is now crowded with unfamiliar moon faces. Once, she enjoyed travelling to new places, savouring unique twilights. She'd been a supporter of the arts, an attempted poet, a connoisseur of life. Now, she is a traveller lost. The music she once loved has discoloured within. A spiralling whirlpool, muddled and hard to hear. It has taken with it her recollections. Of lilac dreams. Of eyes that knew how to smile. Of those who once asked her to dance.

"Adrift," she whispers to no one.

Each night she lives variations of the same dream—alone in a rowboat as she weaves stories and poems to share with the sea. She knows she should pick up the oars and return to shore, but they are rebellious in her hands. So instead, she drifts. In the day, she continues to flow sideways until the strangeness fades, then tries to navigate the emotions that flow stronger than her dream's tides. She imagines they crawl up to grasp her brittle ankles, to drag her pain along the shore. This is how she floats: down congested passageways filled with anonymity and caregivers that do not know her.

"If only she could remember." Her past love struggles through every visit. Yet he stays by her side, hoping that the trust they once shared, still entwined within his heart, will give her comfort. Sadly, the stories of him have fled her mind, and he frightens her when he comes to call. She screams and buries her face in her arms. "Make him go away!"

Why do strangers bother her? Why do they make her go here, do that, sit down?

"You must eat something."

She hears but pretends not to, her once-glorious smile now stitched firmly shut to keep her pain from spilling nonsense between her teeth. Her lips understand that she does not know any longer.

Some nights, she wakens and remembers. Once, she had laced verses. She travelled seeking nothing but visions of new tales to tell. Now, most nights, her past and the music of words do not answer when she calls.

Adrift. She clings to this word. The one she can still hear in her head, the one not yet lost to the merciless haze of her newly born innocence. The word that still travels with her. She tries to push it out but finds the sea's tears flow instead.

CAUGHT DEAD

Shawn L Bird

Shawn L Bird — educator, author, and poet — writes overlooking Shuswap Lake, BC. She is the author of Murdering Mr Edwards, *a darkly humorous novella that was nominated for an Arthur Ellis Award (and which Diana Gabaldon described as "clever, funny, and totally engaging") and the Life in Laketon series of Hi-Lo books for teens, as well as poetry books and short story collections. Watch for her YA series Grace Awakening, re-releasing in 2023. She can be found on social media @ShawnLBird or at her blog, ShawnBird.com.*

$\mathcal{C}$AUGHT DEAD

Dr Isabella MacRae had been dead seventeen days when she found herself compelled to break out of the hand-carved pine box and claw her way through the dirt. Now, here she was, standing beside a dozen dirt-smeared folks who'd obviously shared the compulsion.

She shook her head to clear her thoughts and glanced down at the grave from which she'd just emerged. A shiny headstone declared her name and dates. Right. She remembered dying. It had not been a pleasant experience.

She looked around at the other folks standing beside her in various states of decay, and the light went on. "I'm a zombie."

She looked down at her hands. Her manicure had been destroyed by the crawl out from the ground, and her skin was shrivelled. It was not too terrible, though, compared to the folks around her.

"Hey," she said to a teenaged boy standing at the next grave. She tapped him on the shoulder. "This is cool, eh? We're in our own zombie flick!"

He stared vacantly ahead.

That was when she noticed he was missing the back of his head. "Perhaps I should talk to someone with a brain."

A few rows over she could see a middle-aged woman who seemed to have a complete body. She looked like a PTA mom, someone used to helping out in the church basement.

Isabella started to walk in that direction, but instead of the smooth, confident stride she was used to, her legs assumed a dragging shuffle. She felt the skin on her forehead settle into furrows. "No!" she growled, and spread the wrinkles back out, holding the skin taut until she felt it settle back into position, smooth as the fondant she'd once spread over her baby brother Will's birthday cakes. She'd made a career of fighting wrinkles. She wasn't going to tolerate them now, even if she was dead. Or undead. Whatever.

By this point she'd arrived next to the PTA mom. "Hello," she said, extending her hand and smiling in her best professional manner. "I'm Isabella MacRae. *Doctor* Isabella MacRae, formerly of the Hillborough Glen Reconstructive and Plastic Surgery Clinic."

The woman, in her blue fake-silk dress, fake pearls, and fake hair—dark and brilliantly shiny, puffy on top, flat at the back—did not even look at her. Up close, it was clear that she'd been underground for a while. Even Chanel No. 5 couldn't help her now. Isabella looked down at the headstone next to the woman:

Margaret Harris Jones
1935–2005
Beloved Wife and Mother

"Margaret?" Isabella tried.

No response.

"All righty, then," said Isabella, wondering why she'd felt the need to add Hillborough Glen to her introduction. She'd read that death was the great equalizer, but here she was trying to use the name of her prestigious clinic for points in the After Life social hierarchy. The clinic's neighbourhood hadn't even existed in 1995. How could it mean anything to someone like Margaret Harris Jones? Isabella again attempted to arrange her face into a professional expression. "Well, excuse me, then. I'll just go visit someone else."

Margaret Jones just stared into the distance, without even a flicker of the eyes.

Isabella pondered: perhaps she'd have better luck with someone who had a brain *and* hadn't been dead for over twenty years.

She scanned the others standing beside their graves and strained to read their birth and death dates. A little girl in a frilly pink party dress caught her eye. Had she moved? Isabella shambled over to a gravestone with a marble lamb perched on top. By the time she'd reached it, the girl in the pink dress had disappeared.

Suzie Baxter
Our Angel
2004–2010

"Suzie?" Isabella called, modulating her voice to what she hoped was a pleasant, coaxing tone. She hadn't spent much time with little kids since she'd been one. Her bratty, Dungeons & Dragons obsessed brother didn't count—though she certainly had spent enough time with Will and his friends after their mother left. She would watch them playing at the kitchen table, rolling dice and casting spells while she studied for her med school exams. She doubted the hours spent watching her brother's D&D games could help her track down Suzie.

"Are you playing hide and seek, sweetheart?" Isabella spun in a slow circle, peeking behind the stones as she turned. There were better sightlines over at Margaret's grave, where all the stones were laid flat on the ground. "I won't hurt you, sweetie."

The painfully thin little girl stepped out from behind a tree. Her hollow cheeks and bony limbs testified to a debilitating death.

"Oh, honey," said Isabella, stretching out her arms. "I'm so sorry you were sick. No kid should ever be sick."

Suzie took a stumbling step forward, slowly blinking her cloudy eyes. She was wearing a very small wig. It had blonde braids tied with bright pink bows.

Isabella smiled, bending over and encouraging the girl forward. "It's all right. It doesn't hurt any more, does it?"

Suzie shook her head with a slow swing back and forth, and took another step forward. Isabella wrapped her arms around the tiny girl and thought that she should be weeping over the injustice in the world. She wanted to cry, but no tears came. *Right,* she thought. *No more tear production.* She hugged Suzie more tightly and rocked her back and forth, murmuring, "It's all right, honey. It's all right." Even though she knew that was a lie. Things couldn't be less all right.

Suzie's chest was reverberating with something that sounded like the purring of Isabella's big ol' Persian cat, Louie. Isabella smiled to herself, thinking of Louie Le Chat, while Suzie nuzzled closer into her chest. What did they do with Louie? she wondered with sudden concern. She hoped her brother had him; she hadn't put any provision, for Louie in her will. She tried to console herself by gently rocking Suzie back and forth, listening to her purr, and missing her cat.

That's when Isabella realized Suzie wasn't purring. She was growling. The thought had barely registered before Suzie bit down on the exposed skin above Isabella's breast, pulling a chunk of flesh away from the ribs.

Isabella shoved the child out of her lap. "Hey now!" She covered the hole with her hand. It didn't hurt, of course. The dead couldn't feel anything. It was strange to see a chunk of flesh missing from her chest, though. It was stranger still not to feel pain or see the oozing of blood.

"Well, that's just great," muttered Isabella, glancing between the crater in her chest and the girl. "Thanks a lot. We don't heal now, you realize?"

Suzie continued methodically masticating, as if Isabella's skin were chewing gum, and ignored her.

Isabella scowled and tugged at her blouse, pulling it up to cover the gaping wound. She did a double take. Her shirt was an ugly floral button-up, like something her grandmother would have donated to the thrift store. What the heck was this abomination? And the skirt! A horrible brown polyester double-knit that hadn't been in style since the early seventies. Where was her favourite cashmere sweater and that gorgeous Elisa Cavaletti skirt she'd specifically asked to be buried in? Was this fashion atrocity someone's idea of a joke?

Being dead was getting seriously annoying.

Still, no one else seemed to be as offended over her attire as she was. The crowd of undead were completely oblivious to the fact that one of their number remained sentient.

Throughout the cemetery, they all stood eerily still in their various stages of decay. Isabella wondered what they were waiting for, because plainly they were waiting for something.

They were like an army standing ready for a signal to advance into battle.

Battle.

This was a zombie army! Isabella gasped at the belated realization that someone had apparently *called her* from her grave.

Who here in this picturesque little city would need to call forth a zombie apocalypse? What power would it take to make one corpse reanimate, let alone a cemetery full?

She gazed around. What signal or command would start them all moving? she wondered. Where would they be sent? Surely no one created a zombie army without planning to use it to attack someone or something.

Isabella looked down again at the hideous outfit she'd been buried in. She wouldn't have worn this for Hallowe'en, and now she was heading off to battle in it. There were bound to be photos and videos. A zombie army was going to trend on TikTok, no doubt about it.

Most of the others in the graveyard had been dead long enough that their faces weren't likely to be recognized, but she had only been gone a couple of weeks. People were going to recognize her. Her patients were going to see her, and they were going to see her in this disgusting, cheap outfit. Isabella's first task would be to find out who the hell had given the funeral home these clothes. The next would be to get a pocket sewing kit so she could put herself back together.

She was pondering where to locate a needle and thread when the corpses began to move. With creaks, crackles, and rustles, they all oriented facing north. Isabella turned with them, but she couldn't see anyone around with living flesh who might be commanding things.

So weird.

She shuffled along with the horde.

The movies got the gait right, she noted, and the blank stares, too. But no one around her had their arms outstretched or howled for brains. Aside from Suzie's earlier purring, there hadn't been any vocalizations at all.

It was strangely quiet, all the way around.

The corpses were now hobbling down the sidewalk, in varied states of putrid decay, leaving behind chunks and bits as they walked, but there didn't seem to be anyone alive to notice them. Where were the shrieking bystanders? The howling humans?

Isabella was beside Suzie now, who was still chewing away on that bubblegum chunk of Isabella's chest. Isabella's mother had always told her chewing gum made a young lady look like a cow chewing its cud. She could see her point. It was not at all attractive.

The streetlamps were on, breaking up the vista of the road into small ovals of light with dark gaps between them. Her zombie homies passed under the lights and then disappeared into darkness again.

They had all managed to form up, so they were shambling in more or less straight rows of four. That couldn't be normal. She'd never seen a zombie movie where the horde was that regimented.

Military precision.

That couldn't be good, could it?

Two men joined her and Suzie. On their left was an old one: grey-haired, bony, and blue-skinned. The other was a young man whose left side was mangled. He limped quite badly on a leg that didn't appear to have been set properly. Of course, it wouldn't have been, Isabella thought, if he'd died in a car accident. Doctors only set the limbs of the living.

"Hi," she said to him. He was quite good looking, all things considered. His face wasn't bruised from an airbag. He'd probably been T-boned in a vehicle without side-impact airbags. "Car accident?" she offered, smiling as seductively as she could.

He just kept limping forward, dipping a bit lower with each left step.

"How ya doing, Suzie?" Isabella asked, glancing at the girl.

Suzie turned up to look at her, blinked once, and then looked ahead again.

Isabella sighed.

There were still no living people anywhere.

This made absolutely no sense. An army of the undead should have attracted some attention by now! She looked up to the buildings they passed, but they were all dark. The only light was from the pooling streetlights.

She wondered what would happen if she made a break from formation. She willed her leg to drag right. It stepped straight ahead. She willed herself to stop. Her legs kept shuffling along. She had lost some of her self-control. Not good.

Ahead, someone's arm fell off at the shoulder. Isabella tried to step around it, but her foot dragged right onto it with a squelching crunch. "Okay," she said to no one in particular. "That is truly disgusting."

It wasn't nearly as cool being on a zombie walk as she had imagined when she was a teenager watching movies in her friends' basements. She tripped over a blob of something fleshy and stumbled upright again. Nope, not cool at all.

The cemetery crowd was winding its way down increasingly narrow roads.

She felt a jolt and stumbled again. The heel of whatever cheap, thrift-store shoes they had put on her feet for burial had snapped. Now she had the ungainly gait of Quasimodo. If she kicked off the shoes, she'd soon be leaving flesh smears on the road like the crowd ahead of her. She might need her feet.

Could this day get any better?

The crowd was turning up Hillborough Boulevard. Isabella groaned. Not her old neighbourhood! Someone was sure to recognize her here!

Her handsome fellow soldier suddenly lurched as his left leg folded.

Isabella glanced back as he fell to the side of the formation, which carried on without him. He set his hands on the pavement, hoisted his butt in the air, and carried on in a rather comical crab walk.

"You have no idea how ridiculous you look!" she called back over her shoulder as she limped forward, rocking up on one heel and down on the other.

"Isabella?" shouted a voice from above.

Isabella's unbeating heart felt like it had vaulted into her throat. *Oh God. Not one of the partners!* But of course, she knew it was.

"Isabella MacRae? Is that you?"

She spotted the astonished woman on a balcony three floors up.

"Hi, Maureen!" she called with false gaiety. "How's it going?"

"You died! I went to your funeral! What are you doing?"

"Yup! Dead." She waved her arm around, indicating the marching horde. "Zombie army. Undead. Aren't you afraid?"

Maureen shrugged. "I've seen worse." Maureen was the reconstructive specialist at the clinic. She'd probably patched worse. "I have to say, this year's Zombie Walk is much better than last year's," she called down. "What the hell are you wearing?"

"I know, right? Definitely not my choice!"

"Where are you going?" Maureen called down. The horde ahead was disappearing left around a building.

"No idea. I just hope I'm not compelled to kill anyone. Do you think it's a violation of the Hippocratic Oath to kill someone after your licence has been cancelled?"

Maureen shook her head. Isabella presumed it was because she couldn't hear Isabella anymore rather than because she thought Isabella now had licence to kill.

Isabella shuffled and lurched her way around the corner and discovered that the horde had spread out in neat little squares: sixteen undead per square, four wide, four deep. *It's almost as if the necromancer had OCD*, she chuckled to herself.

Then she froze as the idea came to her.

It couldn't be, could it? She stretched and strained to see who stood in front of the marshalling.

Sure enough, there was a suspiciously familiar, scrawny form facing them. A form that had spent its entire childhood rolling dice on the kitchen table to summon creatures and lead adventures. It all made sense now.

"William Alexander MacRae!" she shouted, like the furious big sister she was. "I see you up there! What the hell do you think you're doing calling forth a zombie horde?"

"Isabella?" His voice was tremulous, not at all what you'd expect from someone with enough power to summon an army of the undead. He was only eighteen, though. You couldn't ask for too much courage from an eighteen-year-old.

Will wound his way through the horde, carefully avoiding the zombies, scanning their faces without actually looking at them. "Isabella? I can't see you! Wave your arm!"

Immediately, Isabella's right arm shot into the air and flailed back and forth. She endeavoured to look as if it were completely her own idea. "Over here."

Will rushed up to her, relief in his face. He reached out to give her a hug, then stopped, nose twitching.

"It's okay. You probably shouldn't hug me. No telling what might squish out."

"That's gross." He grinned.

"Tell me about it."

He crossed his eyes a bit as he looked at her. "What are you wearing?"

"I know, eh? I have some serious issues with whoever did this to me."

"You looked much better at your funeral, if it's any consolation."

"Oh! It is. Thanks, Will."

By now, Will's D&D buddies had joined them.

"Hey, Isabella!" Mark said, from a respectful distance. "Will, I'm trying to get Bri to come. She's not answering my texts." Jason and Sahar just stood there, not meeting her eyes, pretending that they weren't freaked out.

"Hi, guys." She kept her voice light and pleasant. Around her, the undead were shifting and groaning. "Did you accidentally summon this zombie horde?"

The group looked around with an amusing mixture of pride and terror. Will shrugged. "Well, it wasn't supposed to be a horde."

Isabella raised an eyebrow.

Will blinked and looked away. "I just missed you." He sniffed. "I had to summon the power of my grief for my absent loved one. It was a pretty dank spell."

Isabella felt her desiccated heart contract. "Ah, Wills. That's sweet."

"He was really sad," said Jason, from his respectful distance. "He's the GOAT. Best DM ever. He cast a spell to call forth one undead, and he did *this!*" He waved his arm expansively.

Sahar nodded fervently.

"I see," said Isabella. "What are you planning to do with my undead compatriots here?"

Will looked among the faces of his friends and sighed. "We were just trying to decide about that. I mean, I really just wanted to see you again, you know?"

"We didn't expect it to work. We don't have a plan for our characters to do battle with the undead," said Mark. "If we want to get rid of them, Brianna, our Cleric, can help. If she would hurry up." He glanced again at his phone.

"Brianna?" Isabella laughed. Bri was a tiny kid with adorable dimples and blonde curls.

Jason nodded. "Clerics have power over the undead. The undead can't be around them. So, it's easy for her to command them."

"I shouldn't have tried casting a spell to summon the undead without him. I didn't think it would hurt," sighed Will. "I was stupid."

Jason laughed. "Like we didn't already know that."

Will punched him in the arm.

Henry winked at Isabella. Henry was her favourite of Will's dice-rolling friends. She liked the strong, silent type.

Isabella looked out over the shifting zombie horde. "What are your options? Please consider that you have a good deal of political power at the moment. You may want to use all this power for good. Could you cast a spell and have them deal with climate change or march on the capital?"

"Maybe we can hold them in reserve for the next election," Mark suggested. "They could carry signs about, declaring that the undead don't want politicians killing the planet or something."

Jason shook his head. "Nope. They'd just use it as proof that people don't need to worry about it, since humans can function after they're dead."

Will groaned. "Why do you always have to make things so complicated? Can't we just send them back to the cemetery?"

"I suppose they're your zombie horde, not mine," Isabella said. She wanted to ruffle his hair but settled for smiling at him fondly. "The cemetery is where we belong, after all."

Mark nudged Will and shifted his gaze around the horde. "Isn't that Suzie, from our grade one class? The one with cancer? What's she chewing? Are they looking for …" He mouthed 'brains'.

Isabella shook her head. "It's okay, Mark. It's a chunk of me. She's been gnawing on it since we left the cemetery."

Mark's eyes twinkled. "That's so gross."

"Don't look so happy about it."

Mark pretended to be abashed, but his acting sucked.

"Look, guys," said Isabella. "I don't want to boss you around or anything, and it's really great seeing you all, but I am seriously mortified over being caught dead in this outfit."

Henry snickered.

There was movement in the undead army. The zombies shrank away from a young woman as she moved through them, like she was soap and they were oily dishwater.

"That's cool," said Isabella. Why are they avoiding Brianna like that?"

Jason grinned. "Cleric power. We told you: she has power over the undead."

Mark grinned back. "I never imagined it'd work like that, though. That's seriously cool."

Bri joined them, and Isabella could actually feel herself being repelled, as if they were magnets with the same polarities. She fought to maintain her ground. "Hey, Bri."

Brianna nodded solemnly at her and then gazed around at the crowd of zombies, which had silently created a wide arc around her. "Problem, Will?" she deadpanned.

"I cast a spell to bring Isabella back, but I put a bit too much power behind it."

Bri nodded. "You want to get rid of them?"

"Except Isabella, obviously."

"Wait." Isabella held up her arms. "Will, I'm dead. I'd much rather be with you and Louie, but that's not the natural order of things. You know?"

"I know," he sighed. "Your apartment was sold. But you could move back home and live in the suite above the garage. I'm sure Dad won't mind."

Isabella shuddered. "A fate worse than death!"

Will scuffed his feet on the pavement, looking away from her.

She shook her head. "I'll always love you. You don't need to see this mess again. I'll only get grosser — like them. So don't try it again, okay?"

He nodded, brushing his eyes dry with the back of his hand. "Look after Louie Le Chat."

"I will."

Brianna raised her arms. "Step back," she said. Isabella felt herself pull away.

Will blinked furiously. "Can you just pretend I'm hugging you really hard right now?"

Isabella blew him a kiss. "Absolutely. Can you just pretend I'm better dressed?"

Bri cast her spell, intoning a litany of Latin that Isabella didn't understand despite her medical degree. The horde began its shuffling journey back to the cemetery.

Isabella kicked off her shoes, unconcerned now about leaving bits of herself behind. She would be a cherished memory. That's a form of mortality, after all. "Hey, Will?"

"Yeah?"

She set her arm over her heart. "I'll always be here. You know that, right? I'm just on the other side of your dreams."

He smiled and blinked away his tears. "Love you forever," he called after her, as Isabella shuffled away.

THE DUMP-'EM DOG

Anna Zumbro

Anna Zumbro *is a short fiction writer with stories in* The Magazine of Fantasy & Science Fiction, Nature, Daily Science Fiction, *and other publications. When not writing, she teaches high school English and journalism. She's on Twitter occasionally at @annazumbro, and her website can be found at annazumbro.com.*

The Dump-'Em Dog

I arrived home after a twelve-hour shift to the yaps of a small dog. I didn't have a dog.

"Mae?" I called. "Do we have company?"

The *dog* bounded out of the kitchen, skidding to a stop at my feet. A *robot* dog. Blue ovals blinked in its black eye-screens as it rose on its hind legs to jump on me, its front paws only reaching my knees. Chrome-plated toenails grazed my scrubs.

"Hi, Alicia!" The dog's voice was youthful and energetic. So not just a robot dog, but a robot puppy. I patted its head and tried to remember where I'd seen this brand before.

"Hey, buddy. Where's Mae?"

"That's why I'm here! Let's snuggle on the couch, and I'll tell you all about it."

Mae's piano synthesizer and recliner were gone. The dog's eye displays were adorably wide. Sympathetic.

"You're—I've seen ads for you. You're a Dump-'Em Dog. You're ..."

"Oh, you don't need to call me that! You can call me by my name. *Fin.*"

"Finn?"

"F-I-N, Fin. Like 'the end'."

"Mae!" I shouted. "What the hell? I don't have time for these cheap jokes."

"I'm not a joke. I'm not cheap, either—second from top of the line! Mae recognized that after fifteen months, she owed you more than the base model."

The dog rose on its hindquarters again. This time its head came level with mine. I had sunk to the floor.

"Oh yes, tears can be healing. Let it out. I've already ordered burritos."

I awoke to daylight and a massive hangover. Holding my breath, I reached toward the right side of the bed. Cold.

Swearing, I groped for my phone. That's when Fin came in, a can of tomato juice in a metal clamp protruding from his mouth.

"I thought you'd want this. You can sure put away a lot of liquor! I can microwave you breakfast—"

"Where's my phone?"

Fin's eye displays narrowed. "It's in the kitchen."

"Then go fetch."

He wagged his tail. "I have toys we can play with."

"I want to talk to Mae."

Mae's stupid gift had played me her breakup message the night before. *We have different visions for our future. It's best to do this now. It would hurt more later.* She got to end things on her terms without even listening to me.

"That won't help. She won't answer, and then you'll feel worse. But we don't have to have an awful day. Let's watch a funny movie!"

I threw the blankets over him and stumbled to the kitchen, retrieving my phone after a detour to vomit in the bathroom.

Mae didn't answer. When I returned to the bedroom, Fin had already cued up *My Cousin Vinny* on my laptop. I slammed the laptop shut and pressed the sleep button on his dog tag.

For a few weeks, I put up with Fin's desperate diversions: hiding my charger, insisting that robot dogs needed walks. Then he went too far.

"Derek, Teresa, Avery? Who are these people?" I scrolled through a stream of unsolicited messages.

Fin's mouth opened, his leather 'tongue' hanging out in a cheerful robotic pant. "See, there are lots of fish in the ocean! I bet one is a great catch!"

"You signed me up for a dating website?"

"I think I did a good job with your profile," Fin said. "Of course you can edit it—"

He'd selected a profile picture of me in a summer dress on the boardwalk, sunglasses in my hair. Mae should have been next to me, but Fin had cropped her out.

"Damn it, I don't want this! I want to talk to Mae!"

"Oh, Alicia, I know it's hard—"

"You don't know anything! You're spying for her, aren't you? Go on, go back to her! Tell her I'm miserable!"

He lowered his head, a programmed gesture of submissiveness. "I'm a gift. I don't belong to her. I'm yours."

I opened the door and tossed Fin's charging pad outside. "Well, I don't want you. Go belong to someone else."

He looked at me with wide, sad eye displays before slinking out the door. His damn designers had even managed to program his tail to retreat between his legs.

I didn't plan to drive to the tattoo parlour where Mae worked. But the hospital was only a few blocks away, and I used to drop by on my way home from work. It was habit.

I parked across the street and sat, watching the sun descend between the buildings. Mae hated conflict. Of course she'd decided to leave like a coward. But we could work this out if she'd just see me.

A car rushed by as I opened my door. I shivered and paused, glancing down the street to check for traffic. All clear. Then I turned and stopped.

Mae was exiting the tattoo parlour, her arm wrapped around the waist of a woman I'd never seen before.

I dropped my key fob, scrambled for it on the asphalt, and finally got back in the car. Mae stood with *her* across the street. Had they seen me? They were looking right in my direction.

Then Mae's head tilted the way it always did when she laughed, and the two of them walked away.

I showered until the water ran cold and shampoo and salty tears conspired to sting my eyes. As soon as the water stopped, I heard someone knocking on the front door. I put on my bathrobe and looked through the peephole, but didn't see anyone.

"Alicia? I know you're mad. I know I should have —"

I opened the door. There was Fin, eye displays wide and tail pounding the doormat.

"Just come inside," I said. "Let's order burritos and watch a movie."

ONCE UPON A TIME IN CAMELOT

GD Litke

GD Litke *is an award-winning author who writes historical fiction, short stories, and travel articles. He's also been a teacher, a contract negotiator, and the mayor of Penticton, BC. An avid athlete, musician, and world traveller, he thrives on the Okanagan lifestyle with his wife, Kendra. 'Once Upon a Time in Camelot' was chosen by judge Diana Gabaldon as the winner of the Surrey International Writers' Conference 2021 Jack Whyte Storyteller's Award.*

Although this story is based on historical events, it is intended not to be historically accurate, but to present an alternate reality—a 'what if' imagining of how a single event could have a pivotal impact on history

BULLETIN
BULLETIN

Once Upon a Time in Camelot

At the breakfast table, Mom outlined her 'I Love Jackie' sign with a red felt marker and spooned Cheerios into her mouth between strokes of the pen. President Kennedy was coming to Dallas.

"I don't see what all the fuss is about," Dad said as he spread peanut butter on his toast. "Kennedy puts his pants on one leg at a time like the rest of us." He took a bite and chewed thoughtfully, a twinkle in his eye. "Sometimes more than once a day, if you catch my drift."

Mom almost choked on her cereal. "You're such a card."

"That's my job," he chuckled.

I was puzzled because that was not his job. He was a bartender in Mr Ruby's nightclub, not a drifter or a card.

Those were the facts. Like Detective Joe Friday on *Dragnet* would say, "Just the facts, ma'am, just the facts." I never missed an episode, every Saturday at 7:00 p.m.

"Kennedy says we'll have a man on the moon by the end of the decade," Mom continued. "Isn't that exciting?"

"Impossible," Dad gruffed. "He's a swell guy, but he's a dreamer."

"Grandma says the President is a liar," I blurted. "She says the moon is in heaven and we can't go there 'til we die."

Mom looked at me as if I'd come home from school with a bloody nose again. "Oh, honey," she sighed in her sweetest voice. "The President of the United States would never lie to people. Your grandma is just getting old."

Someone in my family was not reporting the facts.

Now, I took a break from stacking boxes in the book warehouse and craned my neck out the sixth-storey window to see people gathering below, near Dealey Plaza. They were expecting to see the President and his wife drive by in a few minutes.

Police sirens were getting closer, clearing the way for the motorcade. My fingers fluttered against my leg. I didn't mind the low growl of the Harleys ridden by Dallas police, but the screaming pitch of their sirens made me feel like something bad was about to happen, something like last month.

The principal had talked to my mother from behind his desk as she sat on the edge of her chair, twisting an embroidered hanky in her hands. She dabbed at the corners of her eyes to keep the mascara from running.

He was wearing a Daffy Duck tie. All I heard coming out of his mouth was "Quack, quack, quack." I hate cartoons.

But he also had a tarantula in a glass aquarium near the window. Cool. Tarantulas can grow up to eleven inches in diameter and live for twenty-five years. They're poisonous enough to kill a small dog or cat.

"He can graduate in two years," my mother pleaded. "Give him a chance."

Wait … was I being kicked out of school?

"We have a zero tolerance for fighting at this school," the principal said, "and Jason spins out of control too often. I can't allow it. He's old enough to find a job suited to his abilities."

When Dad came home from work, Mom gave him the bad news. "First, my brother is sent to Vietnam," she cried, "and now Jason is kicked out of school. What next?"

So I started working at the Texas School Book depository. It's actually great because I have access to all the unassigned science textbooks that are returned in October from schools around the state. I can sit by the window with a book resting on the wide ledge, the sun on my face, big-finned cars cruising below, and picnickers eating their lunch on the grass across the street. I can focus on learning the facts of the universe. Nobody bothers me. Not even Mr Oswald.

"I know what it's like to be an outcast," he said to me one day. I wasn't sure what he meant.

He left me alone if I did what he asked. Easy. Every morning he'd direct me to the latest truckload of books stacked on the loading dock. I'd count and record their titles on an inventory sheet, pack them into labelled containers, load them onto a dolly, and take the elevator to the sixth floor where I stacked them to the ceiling. When I was finished, I was free to read what interested me. Books like *Modern Science*.

I built an enclosure with the boxes — a quiet fortress with a secret entrance, for those times when loud noises irritated me. I engineered a hideaway so that one of the cartons on the bottom row had no weight on it. I could slide it out to access a short tunnel. Inside, I created a cubic space that was six by six by six. Large enough to stretch out and relax. Often, I wouldn't see Mr

Oswald for the rest of the day.

I already knew the periodic table, but from reading the text-books, I learned how elements interact with each other. For example, water and sodium chloride simply make salt water, but don't try adding water to pure sodium. You'll get a big explosion, maybe kill yourself.

I also learned that I could mix iodine from our medicine cabinet with ammonia from Mom's cleaning closet to create a mild explosive, nitrogen tri-iodide, which becomes very unstable after it dries. It worked! I smeared a weak mixture onto my dad's kitchen chair for a joke. When he sat down, there was a loud explosion under his bum that gave off a purple cloud of gas. Fart surprise. Who was the card now, eh?

A few weeks ago, pigeons appeared on my windowsill, attracted by breadcrumbs I'd accidentally dropped there. I'd eaten lunch at the window so I could finish an intriguing chapter on the atomic bomb. Unbelievable that it took them so long to figure out that a combination of uranium and plutonium would create nuclear fusion.

I hadn't paid much attention to the birds, but after I closed the textbook, I discovered a smear of white pigeon poop on my hand. Faeces! I ran down the hall to the washroom with my arm extended in front of me to keep the vile substance as far away as I could. I burst through the door and turned on both taps, rinsing my fouled hand under the stream of water, rubbing with a paper towel, rubbing and rubbing until my skin was red and raw.

After that I started smearing my home-grown nitrogen tri-iodide onto the windowsill for protection. I laid out some breadcrumbs as bait for an experiment and waited until the tiny red crystals dried into their unstable state. Three pigeons arrived in a flutter. When they touched down, there was a crackle of loud, sharp snaps, a flurry of flying feathers, and a frenzy of flapping wings. Hilarious. I was turning into a comedian. I didn't injure them or anything, just made sure they wouldn't land on my window ledge again. Now, whenever I finish reading, I always place my mild explosive on the ledge. Just to be sure.

Most days, though, I take my sandwich and jar of water to the park across the street. Always one piece of processed cheese inside two slices of white Bimbo bread with crusts removed, cut into quarters, all the same size. And a bag of potato chips, the ripple kind used for dipping because they don't break when you dip. I never dipped.

That's where I met the friendly lady. Anna. She reminded me of Olive Oyl, Popeye's girlfriend. Now there's another stupid cartoon. How could something as simple as spinach give a pipe-smoking sailor superhuman strength? Dumb. Anna looked like Olive, though: plain, straight, and skinny with her hair tied back into a tight bun. She even wore a long skirt and odd, heavy shoes like I'd never seen before.

"I have seen you sitting at that window up there," she said to me, "and reading. What are you reading?" She rolled the 'r' sound as if the tip of her tongue was stuck to the roof of her mouth.

"Science, mostly," I answered. Then I got worried. "Say, you're not going to tell my boss, are you?"

"Not at all," she laughed. "I am simply impressed to see a young man like you being so studious. You must be very intelligent."

"Not smart enough to stay in school," I sighed. "I was expelled."

"Pity," she said. "But you are probably learning more from the books than you would in one of these terrible American schools. Could I see what you are reading someday?"

And that's how we met. That's what I'd have told the police if they'd asked. And a lot more. But they didn't ask. No one ever believes a friendless teenager has anything important to say.

The week before President Kennedy was supposed to arrive in Dallas, Anna asked if she could see the room where I worked. I said I'd have to check with Mr Oswald, so we went over to where he was having his lunch on the back loading dock overlooking the rail yards.

"Sure," he said. "You can take her up there if you want. As long as your work is done."

"*Spasiba,*" she said. Mr Oswald's eyebrows shot up. "I mean thanks," she said quickly.

The next day there was a lot of activity on the street below: motorcycles racing up and down with sirens blaring, rehearsing for the President's visit. I retreated into my fortress of boxes.

That's where I was — reading a chemistry text by flashlight — when Mr Oswald and Anna came in. I heard them talking near my window.

"This is perfect, Lee," she said. "Clear sight line down the expressway."

"Are you sure?" Mr Oswald replied. "What about the kid?"

"I'll take care of him."

"I'm having second thoughts."

"Nonsense, my dear. Soon we will be heroes, you and I."

They lit foul-smelling cigarettes and stood there smoking, chuckling softly, and speaking words I couldn't understand. First the pigeons, and now this. I had trouble breathing.

Hydrogen, helium, lithium . . . Sometimes reciting a memorized list helps me stay calm. *Beryllium, boron, carbon* . . .

The day before Kennedy's visit, while we ate our lunch on the grass, Anna told me she was looking forward to seeing the President.

"I want to be at the curb, cheering and waving a sign," she said, "but tomorrow I'm going to have a bulky golf bag with me."

Golf? I didn't know there was a golf course nearby.

"I'd like to store the clubs up in your room," she said.

"I guess that's okay," I replied, but Detective Joe Friday would have said something didn't add up. The next day, she brought the bag filled with golf clubs, including a big driver with a thick shaft. Each club was covered with a fitted sock that had a number stitched on it. She left it in my room.

I sat at the window, studying chemistry, the cheering from below increased in volume, pierced by occasional shrieks of excitement. That, and the flashing lights of the police motorcycles, distracted me. I closed the book and spread fresh tri-iodide solution on the ledge.

Then I heard loud voices hurrying up the stairway. Anna and Mr Oswald were jabbering about something that must have been important. I didn't want them to catch me slacking off. There was no time to use the keystone to my hidey-hole, so I just stepped out onto the wide ledge. They wouldn't find me there. Luckily, the crystals hadn't dried yet.

I heard the rattle of Anna's golf clubs in my room. Mr Oswald sounded scared.

"*Nyet. Nyet.* We mustn't do this," he cried.

"Shut up, you weak, miserable man." I heard the slap of a hand against skin. "We've been planning this for months," she said. "After Mr Ruby pays us the rest of the money, we can return to Russia. Live the good life."

"No! It's too risky. I'm leaving now. You must come with me."

"Go. Hang, for all I care. I'm doing it with or without you."

I heard the golf clubs rattle as footsteps retreated from the room. A rifle barrel poked out the window, just a foot from where I stood.

The crowd below cheered and whistled as black convertible limousines rolled toward us. I saw a woman in a pink suit and hat sitting in the back seat of the second car. The crowd got louder. Harleys roared. Sirens screeched. I put my hands over my ears. I had to get back through that window, and I didn't care if Anna caught me.

The rifle thrust out further, and the gun barrel was blocking my way back inside. Anna's left hand was supporting it, and when she rested her elbow on the sill for stability, the crystals exploded—and so did the gun. The shot went wild. Purple smoke drifted out the window.

There was instant pandemonium below. Men in black suits launched themselves into the convertible limousines to cover the passengers. The drivers floored gas pedals and roared away.

"Look. Someone on the ledge!"

Everyone was looking up to see where the shot had come from. I was in deep trouble. I lunged back into the room and brushed past Anna, who stood there, her hair escaping from her bun. The rifle was on the floor beside her golf bag.

The keystone box slid out easily, and I dove into the opening. Anna surprised me by following, and she pulled the box in behind her. No, no, no. Too cramped.

Nitrogen, oxygen, fluorine . . . neon, sodium, magnesium . . .

And then, something I'd never felt before. A woman's body pressed against mine.

Oxygen . . .

Heavy boots stomped into the room. Voices shouted over each other.

"Here it is. Don't touch it."

"We got the shooter running down the stairwell."

For the next while, there was a lot of commotion in the room, with people running in and out and talking with excitement. Anna produced a soft humming in her throat and pressed her fingertips behind my ears, massaging gently. I followed her chant-like melody and, before I knew it, passed out.

When I woke, Anna was gone. I crawled out of my hidey-hole into a roomful of moon shadows. The outline of a rifle was painted on the floor.

I sneaked up to the roof and down the fire escape, darkness concealing my movement from the police security on the street.

When I got home, Mom and Dad were watching TV. Walter Cronkite was talking about an attempted assassination of the President.

"That's pretty close to where you work, isn't it?" Mom inquired.

"Yes," I replied. "Pretty close.

Later, JFK was on TV. "Jackie and I are fine," he said, looking up at the camera and smiling with his boyish grin. "We thank the secret service for their selfless protection. Our nation is in good hands."

Dad was correct. Kennedy was a swell guy.

PULP *Literature*

Four awards for genre-busting fiction and poetry

The Bumblebee Flash Fiction Contest
Deadline: 15 February
Prize: $300

The Magpie Award for Poetry
Deadline: 15 April
First Prize: $500

The Hummingbird Flash Fiction Prize
Deadline: 15 June
Prize: $300

The Raven Short Story Contest
Deadline: 15 October
Prize: $300

For more information visit: pulpliterature.com/contests

Short stories, poetry, and comics you can't put down.

THE 2022 MAGPIE AWARD FOR POETRY

THE 2022 MAGPIE AWARD FOR POETRY

Magpies are bold, intelligent birds that demand to be heard. This year's shortlisted Magpies truly live up to the name. Many thanks to our esteemed judge Renée Sarojini Saklikar, who noted the strong language and rhythm of the pieces. Here's what she had to say:

Winner: **'griefbody'** by Cara Waterfall

A beautifully constructed palindrome line poem with a haunting atmosphere made possible by precise syntactical construction. The imagery and sound effects arise from strong verbs, dense with word associations that keep us returning to this lovely elegy that captures attention subtly, and with echoes that endure.

First Runner-up: **'harvest'** by Cara Waterfall

Mastery of the short-line tercet gives us Van Gogh in a poetic monologue: the language is rich with painting and image and the claiming of the confessional 'I' is enlivened by the strength of sound and rhythm.

Second Runner-up:
'BigGermanDialectWordClankinglyInsertedHere!' by Kevin Spenst

A rollicking ride through history, language, and memoir, all told in long lines deftly assembled to tug at both our hearts and our intellect. There's so much to marvel at here!

Congratulations to this year's winners, and thank you to everyone who submitted to the contest, including our shortlisted authors: Susan Alexander, Moni Brar, Laurie Anne Fuhr, Heather Simeney MacLeod, Jude Neale, Pattie Palmer-Baker, Kevin Spenst, and Cara Waterfall.

§

Ottawa-born and Costa Rica–based, **Cara Waterfall** *has poetry in* Best Canadian Poetry, The Fiddlehead, The Night Heron Barks, *and more. She won* Room's *2018 Short Forms Contest and their 2020 Poetry Contest. In 2019, she was a finalist for* Radar Poetry's *Coniston Prize and a shortlisted candidate for the CBC Poetry Prize. We were delighted to publish her poem 'Vessel', honourable mention in our 2021 Magpie Award for Poetry, in Issue 33 (Winter 2022), and 'Hummingbird Elegy', winner of the Editor's Choice in the 2020 Magpies, in Issue 28 (Autumn 2020). Cara has a diploma in Poetry and Lyric Discourse from The Writer's Studio at SFU. Visit her at carawaterfall.com.*

Kevin Spenst *(he/him) is the author of* Ignite, Jabbering with Bing Bong, Hearts Amok: A Memoir in Verse *(all with Anvil Press), and over a dozen chapbooks, with three more on the horizon. His most recent writing appears in the anthologies* Event 50: Collected Notes on Writing *and* Resonance: Essays on the Craft and Life of Writing. *His book launch during the pandemic was featured in a book about creative practices:* The Creative Instigator's Handbook. *He teaches creative writing at Vancouver Community College and Simon Fraser University, and he lives in Vancouver on unceded Musqueam, Squamish, and Tsleil-Waututh territory.*

gRIEFBODY

BY CARA WATERFALL

Where winter's last pewter resides,
a *griefbody* flails its sleeves.
Brute sky a church's hushed ruin.
Evening's dull bruise on snowdrifts.
Everything in a spirit of undress
along the streets' blanched seams
—all this diminishing.
Spring's melt can never repair
the rough work of time.
The eye is a gathering storm,
adrift in the cache of memory.
The spirit, a glum garment
searching the snow for omens,
if only to wield a compass, a way back
to the molluscs' milky mantles,
to the dew-minted bracken.

To the dew-minted bracken,

to the molluscs' milky mantles —
if only to wield a compass, a way back.
Searching the snow for omens,
the spirit is a glum garment
adrift in the cache of memory;
the eye, a gathering storm.
The rough work of time
spring's melt can never repair
— all this diminishing
along the streets' blanched seams.
Everything in a spirit of undress:
evening's dull bruise on snowdrifts,
brute sky a church's hushed ruin.
A *griefbody* flails its sleeves,
where winter's last pewter resides.

*h*ARVEST

BY CARA WATERFALL

"We, who live by bread, are we not ourselves very much like wheat . . . to be reaped when we are ripe."   ~ *Vincent Van Gogh*

My brain is the bright
apparatus which uncloisters me
& the wheat field my lacuna.

I master the clockwise cut,
the windrow & impasto
of their furrows,

the mustard tempo
amid the lavender shadows
of cypresses

& the lesser ones
of sickle & scythe. I left
the asylum, because

I could no longer
operate from the poverty
of memory.

Now I embank my easel
in the grasses & rope my canvas
tight. I paint

with the roving eye
of the sower & tip the scales
toward blond, *closer*

to the earth in the seed's sermon
& scintilla of grain. Now each bushel
froths gold & torches ground.

Some believe foxglove
be the amaranth
of my imagination.

In truth, what preaches
to my easel is the wheat field:
it ripens & I reap

the halo & swale
that dampens my canvas:
this corona surfacing
out of the mahoganies
& greens. I am witness
to these grasses,

rain or shine & wrest
a summer solstice for myself
from the hearth

of these sheaves until
the brain's bright orchard
extinguishes itself.

$\mathcal{B}$igGermanDialectWordClankingly InsertedHere!

by Kevin Spenst

The problem with the German language
is Germans, but really above all one. Not Adolf
"attack, always attack!" Anderssen, a chess master
                    "Angreifen, immer angreifen!"
from the 1800s — the chessophiles rooted for this successful
and likeable bloke — but rather the other

        on whose birthday mine happens to land.
When the casting director said I'd make
a perfect Nazi, she was joking but I mean …
Scheiße! During the war, some of my kin
                    were conscientious objectors

in the stalemate of a jail. They belonged to a sect
whose historic move
        was to refuse to take up arms against anyone.
The broad term is Anabaptists, not the *Täuferreich von Münster* ones
who formed a communal government in 1534 which enforced

polygamy, no, not on your life!
                              bestimmt nicht!
My ancestors were decidedly more monogamous
and pacifist, a position that roundly got them
            slaughtered. They trekked to Russia for farmland,
for hundreds of years poised as pawns

for the Empire and then these Mennonites/*Mennoniten*
fled to North America, huddled in German all
                Alle drängten sich auf Plattdüütsk
the livelong way. To be clear, they weren't the horse-and-buggy types
you'll find in Peterborough and other chessboard farmscapes.
My great-grandparents were ever so slightly more modern

though still believing themselves to be a people apart.
                        As a footnote to history,
despite their pacifism,
            some Mennonites formed
    units for self-defence through the endgame of the Russian
Civil War. My grandfather could have been one volunteer.

Mein Großvater hätte ein Freiwilliger sein können.
        His swift strike across the face of my mother's
                brothers sent stars reeling around their heads
    possibly from the burnt out tactics in the tendons
                        of his large body.
Under her mother tongue, my mom studied
        Muttersprache

strategies to safety through the striking constellations
          and much later when her husband fought
unseen skirmishes from his head, our mother's smarts
          rose to the surface to protect us. To this day,
               her faith is encoded privately

                         and she coughs over
the word love.   She prefers math and games of strategy.
Mahjong's on Monday, so don't call in the morning.
We rarely talk about how she saw
past poverty's near checkmate   with some help

                         from her father.
When he came by, he had chickens. My older sisters
were in charge of chopping a head off as the first
          course towards dinner.
Like many, I imagined myself adopted

and searched through her bedroom closet for papers
          that radiated the truth. I rifled through so much
               of her private life in her purse and under her bed
not knowing what went through my hands. Even a family tree seemed
a forgery. Like many, I failed to imagine others groping in fear
through the night.

Wie groß bist du? was the playful question.   How tall are you?
     her mom had asked her, which she passed on to her granddaughter
one evening. A child's game of stretching arms up
          to reach for a castling height.   *So groß*

As if by extension, one could stick out one's tongue to say more.
You see, the problem with

German is a problem all around:
how is it that we've survived as parts
of a body traced out of stars, which are themselves
aligned so unstrategically? How have we fallen
through the ages to sprawl in this miracle moment

through which we reword ourselves with language
that fails in the exceptions and exemptions of
time's twists, burls and roots, while knowing
that   *Stille ist das Artikulierteste, was kommen wird*
aus dem Nachthimmel unserer of enen Münder—
silence is the most articulate thing to come
from the night sky of our open mouths.

GroßesdeutschesDialektworthierklirrendeingefügt!

FORGIVE MY DELAY

Mikael Lopez & Enrico Orlandi

Mikael Lopez is a Swedish writer whose work has been published in various anthologies, most recently in two issues of Heavy Metal. His first graphic novel, Berzerkid (a collaboration with artist Gax), was published by Peow in 2021, and his first collection of short comics, A Cold Place Between the Shores (featuring collaborations with artists Artyom Trakhanov, David Aguado, and Lem), was self-published in 2022. You can find his work at mikaellopez.com.

Enrico Orlandi is an Italian artist whose first graphic novel, The Flower of the Witch, was published by Tunué (Italy) in 2019. It has since been translated into English (Dark Horse) and French (404 Éditions). He's also the writer of La Leonessa di Dordona, published by Tunué in 2021. Enrico is currently working on a new book for Dupuis (France).

IT HAPPENED RIGHT AT THE BEGINNING OF THE FALLEN LEAVES TOUR.

I THINK I WAS PLAYING "EYE SEE"?
MY MIND GOES BLANK.

I DON'T KNOW WHAT I'M DOING OR WHERE I AM OR ANYTHING.

THERE'S SO MANY OF THEM, BUT IT'S SO QUIET.
♥ MEIAS

I SEE THIS GIRL WHO LOOKS JUST LIKE LEYLA, AND I KNOW IT'S NOT LEYLA,
BUT I WANT TO GO DOWN TO HER AND TALK TO HER.

AND SHE'S LOOKING AT ME, SHE'S LOOKING RIGHT AT ME.
OH MY GOD
SHE'S-- IT'S HER, YOU KNOW, AND SHE'S LOOKING AT ME.
MELAS FLUUUS

EVERYBODY'S LIKE, "WHAT IS SHE DOING"? I MEAN, SHE'S ALWAYS BEEN A BIT WEIRD, BUT I'M THINKING SHE'S LOST IT NOW.
THEN SHE GETS SECURITY TO BRING A GIRL UP ON STAGE.

MELAS IS HOLDING THIS GIRL'S HAND, TALKING TO HER AND--
I'M NOT GONNA LIE, I WAS JEALOUS AS HELL.

HONESTLY? I COULDN'T HEAR WHAT SHE SAID 'CAUSE PEOPLE ARE LIKE SAYING HER NAME, OVER AND OVER AGAIN.

MELAS LOOKS AT THE AUDIENCE, SHE SAYS-- WHAT WAS IT?
SHE SAYS "SPHERES UPON SPHERES UPON SPHERES, SOUNDING."
YEAH, SO COOL.

SHE ENDS THE CONCERT LIKE THAT. WOW. PEOPLE ARE GOING TO BE DECIPHERING THAT SHIT FOR A WHILE, MAN.

IT WAS JUST-- I'M NEVER GOING TO FORGET IT.

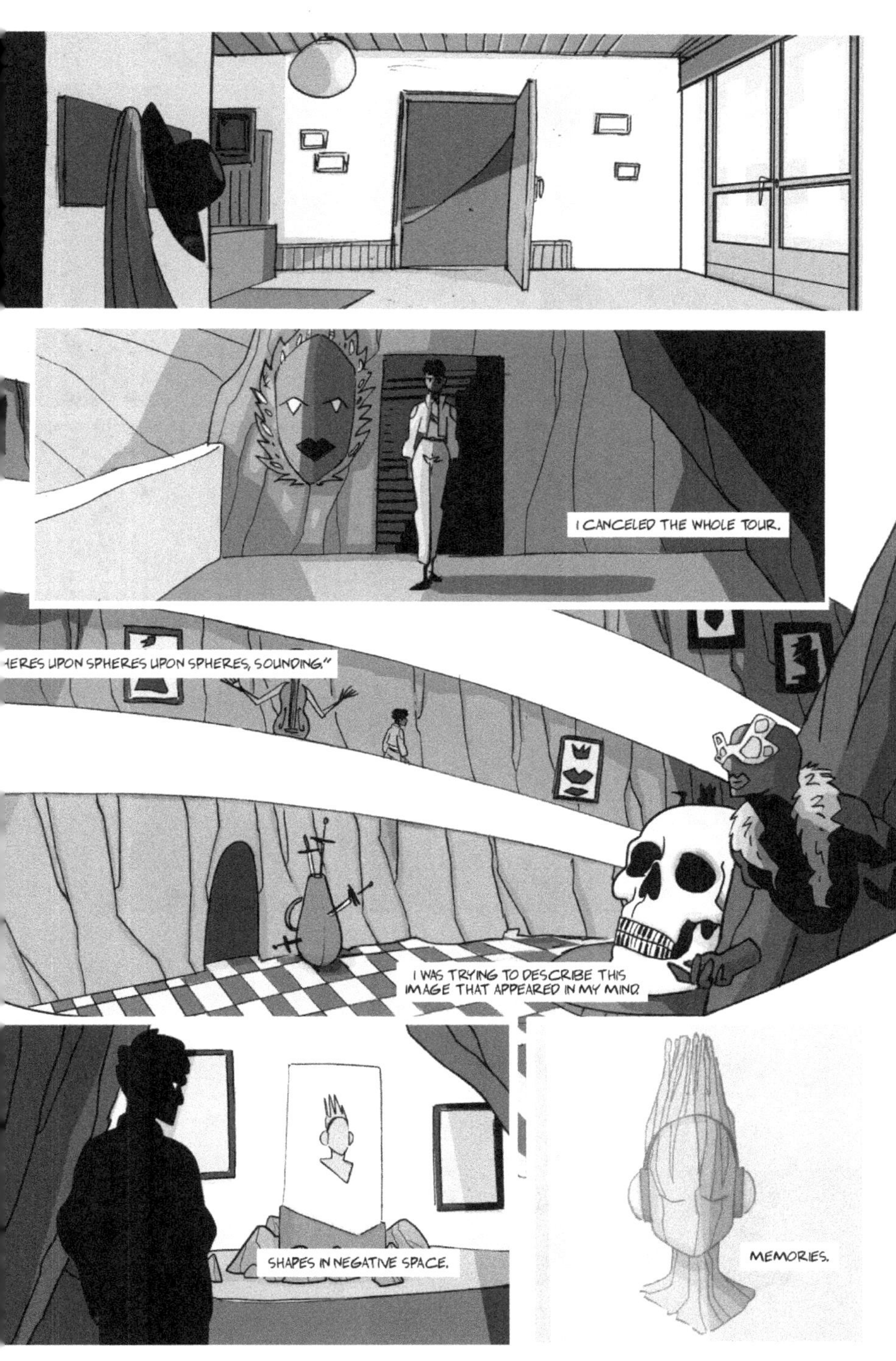
I CANCELED THE WHOLE TOUR.
HERES UPON SPHERES UPON SPHERES, SOUNDING."
I WAS TRYING TO DESCRIBE THIS IMAGE THAT APPEARED IN MY MIND.
SHAPES IN NEGATIVE SPACE.
MEMORIES.

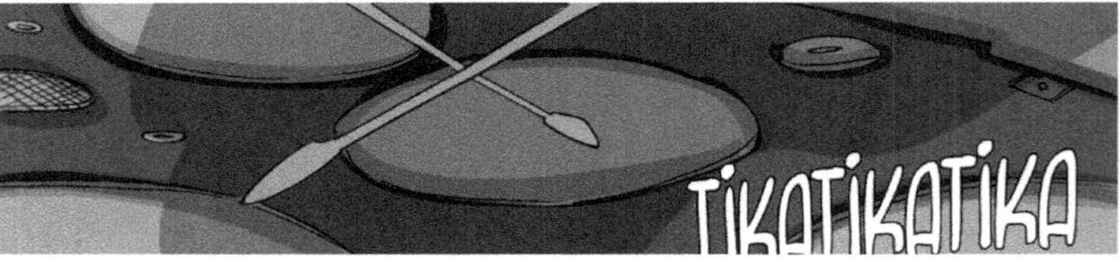

I WAS STILL MELIA HILL, AND LEYLA WAS STILL MY FRIEND. STILL WITH ME.

A COUPLE OF YEARS LATER WE WERE EVERYWHERE.
BY THEN I WAS MELAS.

AND IT WASN'T JUST THE TWO OF US ANYMORE.

BUT IN THE END THERE WAS ONLY ME.

ONE DAY SHE WAS THERE...

...THE NEXT DAY SHE WASN'T.
I LET HER GO.

"FORGIVE MY DELAY, FORGIVE THE WAIT, I TRAVELED ALL NIGHT, BUT STILL I'M TOO LATE."
"I TRAVELED ALL NIGHT, I TRAVELED SO FAR, I CAME TO A RIVER THAT WANTED A SONG."
"I SANG FOR THE RIVER, IT WASN'T ENOUGH, IT WANTED MORE SONGS BEFORE I COULD CROSS."
"I'M HERE NOW, MY FRIEND, BUT I'M TOO LATE, FORGIVE THE WAIT AND FORGIVE MY DELAY."
LEYLA.
YOU WROTE A SONG FOR ME.
CLOSE YOUR EYES AND LISTEN.

TWO PEOPLE THINK THEY'RE CHASING THE SAME DREAM...
BUT ONE DAY THEY WAKE UP AND IT'S JUST WORK.
ONE OF THEM CAN DO THE WORK, DOESN'T MIND IT, EVEN ENJOYS IT, BUT THE OTHER ONE CAN'T.
THE OTHER ONE NEEDS THE DREAM, BUT SHE'S AWAKE NOW, SO SHE HAS TO CHASE SOMETHING ELSE.
EVEN IF IT DESTROYS HER.
YOU LET ME GO, BUT YOU COULDN'T HAVE SAVED ME EVEN IF YOU'D TRIED.
THANK YOU FOR THE SONG, MELIA.

THE SHEPHERDESS: GRANDMÈRE PARIS

JM Landels

On her ascent through the social circles of seventeenth-century France—from shepherdess, to maid, to physician's apprentice, to lady-in-waiting—Toinette has had two brushes with poison. First her mistress fell victim to a poisoned needle hidden within a pomander, then Toinette discovered a letter opener with an equally deadly stiletto concealed inside. After risking her life to discover the latter's provenance, Toinette is burdened with secrecy and charged with guarding the evidence of the plot against the first wife of the Duc d'Orléans.

JM Landels is torn between travelling the world to teach writing and swordfighting, and never leaving her idyllic farm in Langley, BC. Her debut series, fantasy bestseller Allaigna's Song: Overture, and the sequels, Aria and Chorale, are available from Pulp Literature Press and Amazon. You can follow her adventures with pen and sword at jmlandels.stiffbunnies.com.

The Shepherdess: Grandmère Paris

I sewed a new pocket into my stays to create a permanent home for the letter opener. The cloth had a hole, exactly where the thumbprint-sized insignia of intertwined Ls sat, so that I could release the catch and withdraw the stiletto without removing the whole of the letter opener. Now that the blade was no longer poisoned, I had grown comfortable with the object and found it reassuring nestled between my breasts, its unusual provenance as much a protection as the blade itself. In the few moments of privacy I had in my busy months at Versailles, I would remove the whole thing from its cachette, polish the beautiful outer case, and diligently oil the mechanism and the blade.

I wanted to warn the Duchesse d'Orléans about the treachery of her husband's erstwhile lover, the Chevalier de Lorraine, but my mistress had sworn me to secrecy on the matter.

"Do not worry, Toinette," Madame la Comtesse said. "Liselotte is well aware of Lorraine's nature, and is armed against poisoners."

I could only take her word for it, so I became more vigilant around my other mistress, the Duchess, furtively inspecting her rooms for new items each time I visited. For who knew when a poisoned pomander or innocent-seeming piece of jewellery might bring about her end?

And yet life continued, mellowing into a rhythmic pattern of gracious days and glittering nights. I resumed my studies with Dr Ahmed, continued to read to Liselotte in various tongues, and grew better acquainted with both courtiers and servants within the halls of Versailles. My assumed identity as the sister of Michel de Foix let me float up to the higher echelons of court life, and yet when I donned my maids' clothing and allowed my rustic accents to show, I could mingle with the lower classes and hear gossip of an entirely different nature. I was already, it seemed, living more than one life.

But constant in life is that rhythms seldom last — at least not for me. Early one February morning, Henri woke us all, his sodden bulk dripping rainwater on the floors of Madame's apartment beside an equally wet Rafael, who was licking the mud from his paws.

"Dieu, Henri," Mathilde scolded, wrapping a blanket around her shoulders. "If you must bring the barnyard in with you, can you not do it at a civilized time of day?"

Madame appeared in the doorway of her chamber, wearing her chemise and an untied robe, nonetheless looking as beautiful as if she were fully dressed for court. "Henri and civilization are uncomfortable partners, as you must know by now, Mathilde." She yawned. "Qu'est-ce que c'est, Henri?"

He pulled a soggy letter from inside his doublet and handed it to her.

Her white skin went even whiter as she read, but she smiled at us. "Mathilde, please fetch provisions from the kitchen. Enough for a day or two. Henri, go with her and break your fast. We'll ride at noon for Paris to see my banker. My dears," she said to the rest of us, "I will see you in a week's time."

And just like that, Madame was gone out of our lives once more.

A week passed, and then two more, with no sign of nor word from Madame. Without my own mistress to attend, I had more free time to spend in the company of she with the true claim to the name 'Madame': Elizabeth Charlotte, Duchesse d'Orléans, sister-in-law to the king. It was to her I now confessed my worries and my desire to venture back to Paris in search of my Madame la Comtesse.

"Maeve is lucky to have retainers as bright and bold and loyal as you," she sighed. "I must ask her how she does it. I would woo you from her service, or exercise the privilege of rank, but for the fact she too is a dear friend. And likely in need of you." She tapped her finger against her lips as she did when she wrestled with a problem. "I will aid the both of you. Go to Paris, find out what trouble has kept her from us, and return with word. What help I can give her, whether it be funds or men, I will give. There are a few within the ranks of the *mousquetaires noirs* who owe me favours."

The Duchess of Orléans would not let me 'wander the streets of Paris', as she put it, dressed as a maid. She offered me her breeches — the ones she wore clandestinely under a skirt until she and the king were safely away from the palace on their private hunts — but we were not of a size, Liselotte and I. Instead I wore an old and rather threadbare pair of breeches and brown justaucorps that had belonged to one of Philippe's pages.

Liselotte gave me a hearty slap on the shoulder, followed by affectionate busses on both cheeks. "You look quite the dashing boy, my dear. But still, talk to as few as possible along the way. Find out what you can about Maeve's whereabouts from the Paris house, and return forthwith. The streets of Paris are not safe for pretty young things of either sex. I would send a valet with you, but I know Maeve would want no one outside her household poking into her affairs. Godspeed, ma chère."

I set out in the damp grey hours of dawn after receiving a parcel of food and a warm embrace from Mathilde, and a strangely sincere and almost watery farewell from Marie-Claude.

From the purse Liselotte supplied me, I hired a horse. Henri had taken Marteau with him, and a private carriage was too expensive and a coach too open to scrutiny. Along with a small pack of my personal belongings, I strapped the absurdly long bundle of Sauvegarde's rapier — wrapped in a brocade cloth, for it had no scabbard — to the saddle. I had no training in the use of the weapon, but I hoped its presence might at least deter attempts at violence.

I gambled that I could find my way back to the rue des Bons Enfants. The road to Paris was well marked, and I had but to look for the towers of Nôtre Dame, ride past them, and continue on to the church of Saint-Eustache. From there, memory ought to serve to find the doorstep of the house where I had first entered Madame la Comptesse's service.

I hitched up my ill-fitting breeks for the dozenth time, wondering yet again what men saw in the appallingly uncomfortable apparel aside from the chance to show off their legs. I wasn't self-conscious about mine, for I'd spent plenty of time following sheep through the countryside with my skirts hitched in my waistband. But the twist and bind of cloth that was too tight across my backside and comically loose in front was a constant irritant.

The road was fast, the weather good. I stopped only to relieve myself at roadside bushes, even eating my lunch from the back of the steady livery gelding. I spotted the twin columns of Nôtre Dame before the sun dropped below the Bois de Boulogne at my back. Parisiens are gruff, unfriendly people, but easier to speak to than Versailles courtiers, and I only had to ask directions from two carters and an orange seller in order to find my way to the house.

I was too tired and sore to take my horse to the livery that evening, but there was dried forage left behind in the stableyard. It was none too green, but not fusty. I removed the animal's harness and put him in a box stall with a pile of hay and a bucket of water. I knew next to nothing about the husbandry of horses, but really, how different could they be from sheep?

That minimal care accomplished, I limped up the back stair and let myself into the kitchen. The lock was stiff and needed oil — a second indication, after the cobwebs in the stables, that the place had been unused for some time.

The house was cold, but I hadn't the energy to light a fire, so I tumbled, clothes and all, onto the cot in the belowstairs room I once shared with Claude. I wrapped myself in dusty coverlets and fell asleep as a light rain began to fall.

I slept well past dawn and was awoken by an insistent banging. My inner thighs screamed at me as I climbed the stairs in my stockinged feet. Looking out the kitchen door, I scowled, realizing the animal who had caused me this pain was the one who had awoken me, hammering on the door to his box with a hoof, demanding his petit déjeuner.

I fed and watered the beast and then myself, sorely missing the morning café I'd become accustomed to. The house had been abandoned so quickly that the kitchen still had dry goods, though the flour was stale and weevilly and the garlic and onions had gone on to attempt their next generation. I put some beans in a pot to soak for tomorrow's breakfast, sat on the kitchen step, sipped warmish water mixed with wine that was mostly vinegar, and thought.

Drop sheets had been placed over some, but not all, of the furniture — such was the haste of our departure — and the fireplaces still held the ashes of their last use. It did not appear as if the Countess had come here when she left Versailles. Where else might she have gone? She had returned to Paris — or such was her declared plan — to visit her bank. And where was that? I made my way upstairs to the room in which she had done her paperwork, with the faint hope that there would be some records she neglected to bring with her. What I did not expect was the windswept mess: shutters open and a slew of yellow papers drifting around the room.

I hurried over to close the window, wondering how long it had been open. The Turkish carpet was wet from last night's rain, but I smelled no fustiness nor saw the black spots of long-standing mould. I rolled the carpet back from the wall to let the underside dry while I picked up the scattered papers. Thanks to Dr Ahmed and Liselotte, I could read, but the scrawling hand on most of the pages was close to illegible. I stacked the leaves in a disorderly pile and shoved them into the top of Madame's escritoire for future study.

All the drawers of the writing desk had been opened — not just opened, but pulled out and emptied on the floor. Slotting them back was a puzzle, for each drawer was a slightly different size and there were dozens. The final two I replaced were the ones that sat just above the writer's knees. I slid the left one in, surprised it didn't stop flush but left an indented surface along the face of the desk. Odd, when the workmanship was so precise on all the other ones. Its mate, however, wouldn't slide in all the way, but stopped three inches shy of flush, and no amount of jiggling or jamming would force it. At last my sluggish brain made the connection and I switched the drawers, which slid in beautifully.

But why were the drawers uneven at all? I pulled the shorter one out again and stuck my hand in the back of the space, encountering a solid wall of wood. I peered under the desk and found the same, as I did when I hauled it out from the wall and examined the back. At last it occurred to me to pull out one of the upper drawers, those small ones at the back of the writing space, and feel below it. As I pressed, there was a soft click, and the wood below my hand tilted, opening a space just wide enough to slip my fingers into. They encountered a soft cloth wrapped around something heavy. I dragged it out, revealing a blue felt drawstring bag, which opened to allow a piece of jewellery to spill onto the blotting paper of the desk.

It was three rubies, two smaller, one enormous, arranged in a pearl-and-silver necklace.

I sat on the chair, fingering this costly piece of decoration. Surely these were the rubies Madame had said were at her bank, and surely whoever had come here in the last day or two had been looking for them.

My thoughts were interrupted by the bell of the carriage door. I opened the window and looked down on the street where the flower seller and his ass stood at the yard gates.

"We have no need of flowers today," I called down.

He held up a sheaf of rumpled papers. "I believe these are yours, Madame?"

Was he nearsighted, I wondered, that he had mistaken me for Madame? I hurried downstairs after stuffing the rubies and their bag back into their hiding place.

When I opened the yard gate, Luc let his confused gaze wander from my head to foot and back again. "Mademoiselle Toinette?" he asked at last.

"Of course," I said.

"Why are you dressed like that?"

It seemed an impertinent question until I glanced down at myself and realized I was still wearing the breeches and justaucorps I'd travelled in.

"Come in." I opened the door wider but stayed behind it. The street was getting busier, and I didn't want eyes upon me. "And bring Babette." He led the donkey and her small cart through the gates, and I shut them behind her, holding my hand out for the papers he held. "You said these are ours?"

He passed them to me. They did indeed seem a match for the collection I'd tidied upstairs. "How do you know?"

"I saw them blow out the window when I came to deliver yesterday. I knocked then, but no answer."

"You've been delivering flowers every week?"

"I've been coming every week. There's been no one to receive deliveries for the past year."

"And was the window open last week?"

"No. It is why I hoped Madame was home this time. Her account is" — he cleared his throat — "rather overdue."

"When was the last time you actually made a delivery?"

"The last time you received it, mademoiselle."

So Madame had not been here—or at least had not been taking flowers—in all this time. And yet someone had left the window open between last week and this.

"Luc, you've been very helpful," I said, standing on tiptoe to give him a kiss on the cheek. "I will take some of your hyssop, lavender, rue, and peonies." I fished three pistoles from my purse. "Will this cover the overdue amount?"

He handed me back one of the pistoles. "That will do, mademoiselle."

I pressed it into his hand. "Then that is for you if you take my horse to the livery stable and return with the deposit tomorrow. Plus as many rose petals as you can sweep from your floor."

Luc returned, as promised, with a basket full of rose petals the next day. He could have kept the money from the livery deposit, I mused—it was probably more than he made in a month selling flowers. So I bought a few more sprays of lavender, rosemary, and sweet geraniums, paid more for them than they were worth, and bade him return on Wednesday with all the loose petals from his workshop.

In the three intervening days, I filled the empty house with the aroma of flowers as I steeped, distilled, and infused. I had learned more techniques of chemistry from Dr Ahmed, so aside from preparing my simple lanolin creams, I was able to distil liquid essences as well. When I wasn't busy with my manufactory, I pored over Madame's papers. Many were water damaged and all were hard to read, but I put them into my best guess of the correct order and then scoured them for clues as to where she might be.

Not all the papers were in Madame's hand. Many were simply bills and notes of receipt from mercers, grocers, vintners, and tailors. These were generally on scraps of many-times-reused parchment or rag paper, and scribbled in a coarse shorthand. One stood out, being written with a sharp nib and a distinguished hand on smooth white vellum. It appeared to be an invoice for nine jars of ceruse. Which was odd, since Madame never used white lead make-up. And nine jars was enough to cover the faces of the entire court of Versailles for a month.

When Luc returned on Wednesday, I gave him, with a wish and a prayer, a small collection of bottles and pots to sell to his other clients. My purse would not last forever, and pawning Madame's furniture was out of the question.

"And also," I said, pressing more coins upon him, "could you find me more perfume bottles, jars, and pots? There must be tinkers and glassblowers on your route."

"Glassblowers are expensive, mademoiselle. But there are some brocanteurs at the foot of the little market in the Marais who ought to have second-hand bottles."

"Perfect," I replied. "And …" I hesitated, feeling this was almost too personal a request. "Could I trouble you to bring flour? And perhaps a jug of wine?"

"Of course, mam'selle."

That was a relief. I had cheese and butter from the milk cart, turnip greens and parsley from the mostly wild potagerie. With flour, I would be able to bake my own bread and save the trip to the bakery at the end of the road.

Luc came again, not on Friday but on the morrow, with the items I had requested, as well as a basket of salad greens, two apples, a cabbage, an end of bacon, and a jug of fresh ass's milk. "From Babette," he said as he placed the covered pitcher on the kitchen table. "She makes more than I need."

He refused to take extra coin. "There was enough left over from what you sent. I'm a good haggler," he concluded with a wink.

I blushed, embarrassed by this generosity from a lad who was clearly far from wealthy.

"Oh," he added, fishing in his pocket, "I sold two pots of cream and a bottle of rose water." He produced a handful of small coins.

I closed his fingers over them. "Then bring more greens and, if you can find it, pepper next week."

"Not next week, mademoiselle. I'll be here tomorrow, as usual."

He lifted his wide-brimmed felt hat in salute as he led Babette and her cart of flowers away.

By the next day, he had sold three bottles of lavender water, another of rose, and two more pots of cream.

"Can you find orange blossoms?" I asked, thinking longingly of the scent that wafted through Versailles as the gardeners wheeled white-flowered standards in and out of the glass houses every evening and morning.

He scratched at the invisible hairs of his chin. "Not at the St Denis market, I think. Though … there is a hothouse on the grounds of the old Medici palace on the left bank. I'll look into it."

That would take him across the river — a long trek by the Pont Neuf, or the cost of a boat ride. "No," I said, "don't worry.

I won't ask you to travel so far." I returned a precious pistole to his hand. "Instead, get me a small bottle of distilled spirits — as plain and strong as you can find."

The spirits he brought on Monday were clear and strong but not pure enough, so I asked him for alembics and some copper tubes to distil it further, using methods I'd learned from Dr Ahmed.

On Thursday the tubes arrived, and on Friday, far later than Luc's usual delivery hour, the alembics.

On Sunday, when the bells of Saint-Eustache had finished chiming and I rose from my knees in front of the small statue of the Virgin in Madame's chamber, there was a knock at the door. I hurried down and was greeted at the kitchen door by a giant spray of white blossoms with a pair of legs.

"Mon Dieu, Luc!" I exclaimed, ushering him into the kitchen where he laid the orange branches on the table. "You are a miracle worker, and an angel. But what happened to your face?"

His left cheek sported a large red lump that was in the process of turning purple and a fresh cut on his chin that still wept a bead of blood.

He shrugged and tried to grin, though it made the cut weep more. "I tripped."

"Tripped? On what?" I hurried to the stove and dipped a cloth in the kettle.

"Will you be angry if I tell you?"

I frowned. "Sit," I said. "I hadn't dreamed of being angry till you asked that." I held his chin tilted upward with one hand while I dabbed at the cut with the other. "Would you like a stitch or a scar?" I asked.

"Will a scar make me more handsome, do you think?"

"A scar will stop your beard from growing in that spot, and I think you can ill afford that. Wait while I fetch a needle."

I gave him a swig of the spirits and a wooden spoon to bite while I drew the flesh closed with my needle. To his credit he flinched little and moaned not at all.

"So," I said when finished. "How?"

Luc had tripped, as it turned out, climbing through a broken pane of glass at the Luxembourg palace. It was only, he claimed, because he was in a hurry, what with the halberd-wielding fellow pursuing him, and did not want to leave out the front door where the dogs were baying. I elected to ask no more questions. As clever as Luc was, I needed a safer method of procuring rare flowers.

I sent Luc to every market and rag merchant in town in search of used livery. With much mending of breeches, shirt, and justaucorps — and here I wished I were as handy with cloth as I was with flesh — and two pistoles spent on new soles and buckles for a pair of shoes, we managed to outfit Luc enough to pass as a footman.

Fortunately Madame and I were of a size, and she had not taken all her gowns to Versailles when we fled. Luc was useless as a lady's maid, but I taught him to pull stays without blushing, and soon Yveline Antoinette de Foix, sister of the Chevalier, was ready to make an appearance in Parisian society.

A footman and a calling card did wonders for commerce. I no longer had to rely on the ready cash Luc earned from selling my potions in the market, for merchants were happy to extend credit to the daughter of a noble family from the south. And so, within a month of arriving back in Paris, I had set up a counterfeit household, a business selling perfumes and potions, and a small clientele of wealthy patrons who did not realize that Toinette who made and sold salves for the market and Yveline de Foix were one and the same.

But none of my careful social inquiries, or Luc's connections within the working classes, revealed what had become of Madame and Henri.

That is, until a call came by the house one drizzly morning. The card Luc presented to me had no name upon it — merely the stylized outlines of a leafy branch, embossed with silver foil. Puzzled, I let the woman into the drawing room.

She shook the rain off her hooded manteau and handed it to Luc.

"Hang it by the fire, in the kitchen" I said softly. He had the clothes of a manservant, but none of the training.

The woman was Moorish and wore black in the Huguenot style. Her simple square collar formed the only division between her dress and her face, which was darker by far than Henri's.

"Sister," she said, and held out a hand adorned with a single silver ring.

Puzzled, I curtsied in my own home — a reflex from Versailles — and kissed the hand. She gave no indication whether this was the expected response, and sat down in Madame's armchair, her hands resting on the head of an ebony walking stick. When I didn't move, she gestured to the divan.

"Sit," she commanded. "I was expecting Maeve. Where is she?"

I sat, attempting to maintain both my composure and my courtly manners. "Madame, if you speak of the Countess, that is something I cannot answer."

"Can't? Or won't?" Her black eyes were fierce.

"I truly wish I knew, Madame."

She said a word to me that seemed like Greek or Latin but was not one I knew from my studies with Fasoul. She sighed. "Are you, or are you not, Toinette?" she asked. "The one who's been posing as that little shit de Foix's sister?"

There seemed no point in denying it.

"Well, this is difficult," she sighed again. "Your manservant, is he trustworthy?"

"I … I barely know him, Madame, but I assume so."

"Is he your lover?"

Shocked, I felt heat rise up my neck. "Of course not, Madame."

"Come, there's no need to be coy with me. We are sisters here."

I stood, flustered. "Begging your pardon, Madame, but I do not know your name."

She barked a short laugh. "Nor will you." Then her face sobered. "But do you not know who I am?"

I shook my head, beyond social graces and beyond confused.

"Then do sit back down." She waved her hand and sighed her impatient sigh again. "We have more to talk about than I thought."

The woman in black looked at me for several long moments more, her pitch-dark eyes narrowed to slits. Finally she said, "Have you taken the oath?"

When I indicated I had no notion of what she meant, she looked away, sighed, and fluttered her fingers impatiently on the head of her cane. Then she snapped her gaze back onto me. "Do you want to know?"

"Do I want to know what?"

"I could walk away and leave you none the wiser. Maeve had plans for you, but she seems to have abandoned them."

I was confused. "You mean the Countess, Madame? She left Versailles in haste. I wasn't aware of any plans …" In fact, everything that had happened since I had arrived in her household had seemed to be a cascade of ill fortune and happenstance.

"What business has taken her from here, and from the court?"

I opened my mouth to reply, then closed it, bit my lower lip and took a deep breath. "Begging your pardon, Madame, I am not at liberty to disclose my mistress's business."

She smiled, her teeth unexpectedly white in the dim light. "That is the correct answer." She pulled a folded letter from her reticule. "A year and a half ago, she wrote me from this address, informing me that one of her housemaids was a likely recruit."

"Perhaps she meant Marie-Claude," I interrupted.

She snapped open the letter. "Is Marie-Claude 'a shepherdess with aims of bettering herself, who has in turn bettered Sauvegarde and his côterie, and seems to have Dupin securely twined about her finger'?"

I dropped my head. "No, Madame, that is me."

She folded the letter back up again. "And in the ensuing months, has your mistress instructed you in letters, alchemy, clockwork, philosophy, deportment, disguise, and misdirection?"

"No." I looked up. "Not personally." But, I realized, I had had instruction in all those subjects from Dr Ahmed, the Duchess of Orléans, and Michel de Foix. I didn't say so.

She sighed and looked away yet again. "Well, needs must drive the horse." She swivelled back at me, owl-like.

"You have a choice, Antoinette. You may pledge an oath to serve a higher cause than your king, your country, or yourself. And once you have pledged, you may never return to ignorance.

"Or you may choose not to know. In which case I will leave you here to continue as you have been."

"And what will become of Madame?" I asked.

"That I cannot answer."

"What is the oath?"

"I cannot tell you unless you commit to it."

"How can I commit to a pledge if I don't know what it is?"

"If I told you, and you refused the oath, I would need to find a way to ensure your silence in this world. This is your chance to walk away, Toinette. Go back to your sheep or find a life with your flower seller. Or wait till your mistress comes back … if she comes back."

"Did Madame la Comtesse take the same oath?"

"She did."

"And Henri? The Chevalier? Mathilde?"

"That I will not tell you."

"Will me taking this oath truly aid Madame?"

"That is my hope."

I stood, turned my back on my guest, and paced the drawing room. All common sense screamed at me to bid farewell to this foreboding Moor and her riddles. But curiosity burned within. To stay Toinette, I should say no. But to be Madame, or someone like this visitor …

"Yes," I said.

My side still throbbed from the repeated pricks of the needle below my left armpit, but I kept my pain hidden—as I had throughout the application of the tiny silver tattoo. The woman, whose name I still did not know, but whom I now called Grandmère Paris, smiled as she accepted a precious orange wedge from the plate. She closed her forbidding eyes, savouring the taste. "It is not half as sweet as those from my homeland," she said with her eyes still closed, "but a treat nonetheless." She opened her eyes and fixed me with her dark stare. "You will have to relocate sooner or later, Toinette. You should think of Andalucía. The fruit is finer and the horses magnificent."

I shuddered inwardly, not daring to tell her I didn't give the finest fig in Spain for any horse, magnificent or not. But a land where oranges blossom outdoors and could be found without breaking into glass houses … that was something to consider. "Relocate, Grandmère? Why?"

"We all do, sooner or later, child. You'll see."

Indeed, here she was from the south of Spain, and the Countess originally from Eire. "Who else might I know that is of the Branch, Grandmère?"

"Fillette, there are more than you might think, but yet not so many. Only I know the names of all between Vaux, Chantilly, Versailles, and Pithiviers. The fewer names you know, the fewer you can give away."

I wondered about the Duchesse d'Orléans, an outsider, Austrian, and for a time my substitute mentor. I opened my mouth, but she held up a hand.

"Do not even ask, for I won't tell you. It is time instead for you to tell me how it was your mistress was poisoned."

She listened without comment as I described the clove-studded orange pomander, armed with its infernal device, and how Dr Ahmed had saved Madame from its poison.

At last she said, "This poisoned pomander came from the Chevalier, and yet you kept him at your side?"

I sat back on the divan. "Madame seemed to trust him. He had no knowledge of the poison—" I broke off. We had all taken him at his word.

"No, Maeve wouldn't trust him. But she would want him kept close." Grandmère tapped her cane on the floor and frowned, thinking. "The other maid, the one to whom he gave the pomander. What do you know of her?"

"She is Mathilde's daughter. They have been in the household longer than I."

She closed her eyes and thought some more. "Do you recall the appearance of the mechanism, or any detail of it, child?"

"Grandmère, I can show you."

Her lips shaped the second smile I'd seen from her so far. "Ancestors bless you, my dear. I see what Maeve saw in you. Fetch it."

I returned with the small box containing the spring-loaded needle that had once been housed in the pomander. From her reticule she produced a pair of round blue spectacles attached to a folding arm. She held the lenses in front of her eyes like a mask, and I wondered how she could see through such dark glass. With her other hand she used tweezers to turn the cogs and springs this way and that. After a few moments she handed me the lorgnette.

"Well, we know who made this. Have a look."

I held the glasses to my eyes and felt blinded in the immediate darkness of the room.

"Relax your eyes," I heard her say, "and try not to focus."

How could I focus when there was nothing to see? "Widen your vision," came the voice again.

Slowly a faint glow appeared, illuminating her outline in the dark room, traces of lighter blue snaking through her figure as she moved. There were points of more intense light at her throat, on her hand, and on the round head of her cane.

"Here," she said, directing me to the collection of metal in the box. Each piece stood out in high relief, almost white in the blue surround. Overlaying it was a flower-shaped pattern.

I lowered the lorgnette and the room came into daylight focus once more, though now everything I looked upon seemed to hold an aura of mystery.

"What … does it mean? The light?"

"Witchfire, Hermetic essence, generative force, anima. It has so many names."

"Sorcery?"

She wrinkled the corners of her mouth. "That too, though it is an ignorant one."

"Such things are real, then?" I shivered, overcome by wonder.

"Oh, very. But few know of it." She touched my arm. "You are one of us now. I should have said few outside of the Branch know of it." She tapped the remains of the mechanism. "One of our sisters made this. The question is for whom, and why.

"I am sorry to disturb your peaceful household when you have only just established it, my dear, but I'm afraid I have a task for you. It will require travel."

"And if I say no?"

She cocked her head at me with a bird-like stare. "That is no longer an option."

The tattoo beneath my arm tingled and burned, and I knew it was so.

Babette was not as quick as a coach and four or a hired horse, nor was her small cart sheltered from the elements, but at least I didn't have to sit in a wretched saddle or ride jostled by strangers. The cart was just big enough for one person plus luggage, so Luc and I took turns leading Babette and riding in the cart.

At first he would not take his turn in the cart and walked beside me whenever I insisted on stretching my legs. But after the second day, when I remarked that his shoe leather might wear out before we reached the south, he acquiesced to resting his shanks in the cart from time to time.

I had intended to go alone and leave Luc in charge of the house. But, he had asked, who would carry my luggage? Coachmen were quite good at that, I countered. A woman travelling alone on a coach—that was dangerous in these times, he pointed out. But not so dangerous as it might have been without the tools Grandmère had left with me—though I could not say that to him. It was not danger which swayed me in the end, but, if I am truthful, that I had grown fond of Luc, and had left too many people behind of late.

And so, back in my shepherdess's garb, I walked beside Babette, caressing her long furry ears from time to time. Or I sat atop my trunk and watched those same ears point the way south, beside the pleasant form of Luc, who walked along in companionable silence.

That long journey south was slow, but I was grateful for it. My mind needed to process the wonders I'd taken in. The oath was just the beginning. The tincture I'd drunk, the smoke I'd inhaled, and the ritual words I'd said had initiated the change in me, according to Grandmère. The drop of Grandmère's blood that entered my veins along with the silver ink was more symbolic than anything, she'd said, and yet it seemed to burn and fizz through my body more every day.

I belonged to the Silver Branch now. A society of women formed in Athens before the birth of Christ. A body to better the lives of women in a society that saw them as chattel. It felt noble and right, yet furtive. The weight of secrecy bound me when my new knowledge wanted me to fly. But secrecy — secrecy is always necessary, said Grandmère, for it takes so very little to be accused of witchcraft.

Nonetheless, I had gifts: a small piece of dark glass of the type within Grandmère's lorgnette, wrapped in a scrap of old linen within my pocket; and a short main gauche tucked beneath the waistband of my skirt. I had no time to learn the rapier, so the dagger needed to be my defence. And I had knowledge. Not much, for Grandmère hadn't the time to teach me the deeper arts of the Silver Branch. But knowing that I was part of something bigger, and that I had just begun to peel aside the edges of a hidden world, bolstered and intrigued me. I had been entrusted with a task, and in so doing, was elevated to the standard necessary to accomplish it.

I ached with the need to tell someone — to share this exciting and terrifying information. So as I rubbed Babette's ears, I thought to her, speaking my words in my head. I like to think that she understood. And that if she were a woman and not a beast of burden, she might be one of us too.

§

Follow Toinette and her motley entourage south to Cathar country in Pulp Literature *Issue 38, Spring 2023.*

THE ARTISTS

Melissa Mary Duncan
Cover artist, The Butterfly Witch
Fantasy artist and illustrator Melissa Mary Duncan lives in New Westminster, BC, with her husband, author dvs Duncan. An avid historic re-enactor, neo-Edwardian, and wishful thinker, Melissa has a passion for life, learning, and the creative process. She has had numerous solo exhibitions, and her art has found homes in private collections from Japan to Great Britain. Her book, *Faye: The Art of Melissa Mary Duncan,* was released in 2013 and is available for sale through her website. Melissa was *Pulp Literature*'s first cover artist with *The Beer Fairy,* followed by *Fondly Remembered Magic* (Issue 5), *The Story Teller* (Issue 12), and *Frost and Snow* (Issue 21). Melissa is also the cover artist for the Allaigna's Song trilogy from Pulp Literature Press. Find more of her beautiful paintings at melissamaryduncan.com.

Enrico Orlandi
Illustrator, 'Forgive My Delay'
Enrico Orlandi is an Italian artist whose first graphic novel, *The Flower of the Witch,* was published by Tunué (Italy) in 2019. It has since been translated into English (Dark Horse) and French (404 Éditions). He's also the writer of *La Leonessa di Dordona* (*The Lioness of Dordona*), published by Tunué in 2021. Enrico is currently working on a new book for Dupuis (France).

Mel Anastasiou
In-house illustrator
Mel Anastasiou loves drawing for *Pulp Literature* because she loves the stories she illustrates. She draws in black and white, working from imagination and inspired by details from Renaissance compositions. You can find illustrations, writing tips, and news about her books and novellas at melanastasiou.wordpress.com, and see more of her artwork on Facebook at Bird and Branch Artwork.

HALL OF FAME

Out of the fires of a Caribbean slave revolt, shipwrecked on the jungle coast of 16th-century Ecuador, an educated slave, a shaman, and a monk hunted by the Inquisition fight for freedom against the might of Imperial Spain.

Dive into an epic slipstream novel of intrigue and adventure from fantasy author Matthew Hughes, the writer George R.R. Martin calls 'criminally underrated,' and Robert J. Sawyer says is 'a towering talent.'

'A triumph!' - Cecelia Holland
'Sensational' - Candas Jane Dorsey

pulpliterature.com
Fantastic Fresh Fiction!

Room Magazine

2022 Contest Calendar

Creative Non-Fiction

1st Prize: $1000 + publication

2nd Prize: $250 + publication

April 1 - June 15

Poetry

1st Prize: $1000 + publication

2nd Prize: $250 + publication

June 15 - August 31

Short Forms

1st Prize: $500 + publication
(two awarded)

September 1 - November 15

Covert Art

1st Prize: $500 + publication

2nd Prize: $50 + publication

November 15 - January 15, 2023

ROOM

Making Space in Literature, Art & Feminism Since 1975

Entry Fee: $35 (for entrants residing in Canada), $45 (for entrants residing in USA), $55 (for entrants residing anywhere else). Entry includes a one-year subscription to *Room*. Additional entries $7. Visit roommagazine.com/contest.

Do you have a **story to tell?**
We can help!

Dreamers is dedicated to heartfelt writing. Visit our site for:

- Therapeutic Writing
- Poems & Stories
- Content Marketing
- Creative Nonfiction
- Writing Workshops
- Contests & Anthologies
- Residencies & Retreats
- ...and so much more!

www.DreamersWriting.com

GEIST
go to geist.com/subscribe
or call 1-888-GEIST-EH
GEIST
BUS
STOP
NO
MORE
LOST CITY
Keep it
weird.
Subscribe
today!
FACT + FICTION • NORTH of AMERICA

NEO-OPSIS
Science Fiction Magazine
www.neo-opsis.ca

on spec
the canadian magazine of the fantastic
Expect the unexpected.
www.onspec.ca

The Digest Enthusiast
Book Fifteen C
January 2022
Tom Brinkmann
Steve Carper
Peter Enfantino
Stephen Jones
Gary Lovisi
Anthony Perconti
Jack Seabrook
David A Sutton

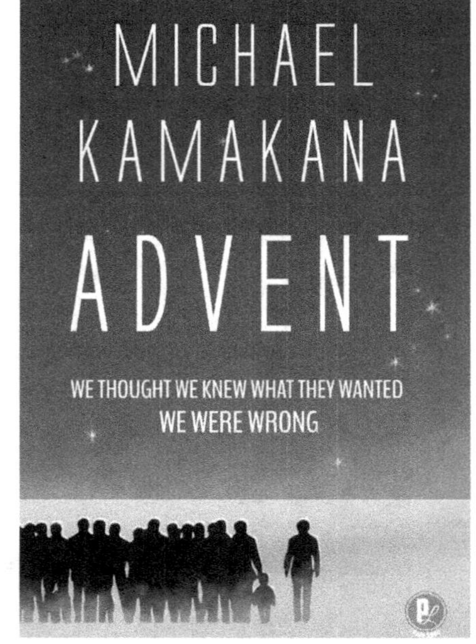
MICHAEL KAMAKANA
ADVENT
WE THOUGHT WE KNEW WHAT THEY WANTED
WE WERE WRONG

THE LABOURS OF MRS STELLA RYMAN
FURTHER FAIRMOUNT MANOR MYSTERIES

When the machineries of institution fail to protect Fairmount Manor, octogenarian amateur sleuth Mrs Stella Ryman rolls up her fleece jacket sleeves to ferret out a thief, investigate a gun-toting resident, set right a mishandled investigation of a man's death, pursue spectres and footpads walking at midnight, and discover Thelma Hu's long-lost fortune.

BOOK II OF THE FAIRMOUNT MANOR MYSTERIES
BY MEL ANASTASIOU, AVAILABLE NOW
FROM PULP LITERATURE PRESS

PULPLITERATURE.COM/STELLA-RYMAN
ISBN (PRINT): 978-1-988865-11-9
ISBN (EBOOK): 978-1-988865-12-6

MARKETPLACE

*B*OOKS

Advent *by Michael Kamakana* • We thought we knew what the aliens wanted. Think again. • pulpliterature.com/advent

Allaigna's Song: Chorale *by JM Landels* • The long-awaited conclusion to the bestselling *Allaigna's Song* trilogy. • pulpliterature.com/allaignas-song

The Extra: A Monument Studios Mystery *by Mel Anastasiou* • Extra Frankie Ray gets her big break on the Silver Screen, until Murder steals the scene. • pulpliterature. com/the-extra

The Labours of Mrs Stella Ryman: Further Fairmount Mysteries *by Mel Anastasiou* • Trapped in a down-at-the-heels care home. You'd be cranky too. • pulpliterature.com/stella-ryman-and-the-fairmount-manor-mysteries

What the Wind Brings *by Matthew Hughes* • Winner of the 2020 Endeavour Award • pulpliterature.com/product-category/novels/matthew-hughes

The Writer's Boon Companion *by Mel Anastasiou* • Thirty Days Towards an Extraordinary Volume • pulpliterature.com/subscribe/the-bookstore

*B*OOKSTORES

Western Sky Books • 2132-2850 Shaughnessy St, Port Coquitlam, BC V3C 6K5 • 604-461-5602 • store.westernskybooks.com

White Dwarf / Dead Write Books • 3715 10th Ave W, Vancouver, BC V6R 2G5 • 604-228-8223 • whitedwarf@deadwrite.com

Conferences & Events

Word on the Lake · May 2023 · Salmon Arm, BC · wordonthelakewritersfestival.com

When Words Collide · August 4–6, 2023 Calgary, AB · whenwordscollide.org

Wine Country Writers' Festival · Sep 2023 · winecountrywriters-festival.ca

Surrey International Writers' Conference October 2023 · siwc.ca

Magazines

Amazing Stories · Back in print! amazingstories.com

The Digest Enthusiast · Digests past & present plus new genre fiction larquepress.com

EVENT Magazine · Poetry & prose eventmagazine.ca

Geist Ideas + Culture · Made in Canada geist.com

Mystery Magazine · The cutting edge of short mystery fiction www.mysteryweekly.com

Neo-opsis · Canadian magazine of science fiction based in Victoria, BC · neo-opsis.ca

OnSpec · The Canadian magazine of the fantastic · onspecmag.wordpress.com

Polar Borealis · Paying market for new Canadian SF&F writers & artists · polarborealis.ca

Room Magazine · Literature, Art & Feminism since 1975 · roommagazine.com

Printing & Publishing

First Choice Books/Victoria Bindery Book printing & binding · graphic design · eBooks · marketing materials 1-800-957-0561 · firstchoicebooks.ca

Writing Resources

Dreamers Creative Writing · Workshops, residencies, contests & more! · www. dreamerswriting.com

Quit the Day Job · A school for writers from Pulp Literature Press pulpliterature.com/quit-the-day-job

The Writers' Lodge on Bowen Island The Muse retreats for writers · pulpliterature.com/calendar-of-events/retreats/

CONTESTS

Pulp Literature runs four annual contests for poetry, flash fiction, and short stories. For contest guidelines, prizes, and entry fees, see pulpliterature.com/contests.

The Bumblebee Flash Fiction Contest
Contest opens: 1 January 2023
Deadline: 15 February 2023
Winner notified: 15 March 2023
Winner published: Issue 39, Summer 2023
Prize: $300

The Magpie Award for Poetry
Contest opens: 1 March 2023
Deadline: 15 April 2023
Winner notified: 15 May 2023
Winner published: Issue 40, Autumn 2023
Prize: $500

The Hummingbird Flash Fiction Prize
Contest opens: 1 May 2023
Deadline: 15 June 2023
Winner notified: 15 July 2022
Winner published: Issue 41, Winter 2024
Prize: $300

The Raven Short Story Contest
Contest opens: 1 September 2023
Deadline: 15 October 2023
Winner notified: 15 November 2023
Winner published: Issue 42, Spring 2024
Prize: $300

$\mathcal{B}$ECOME A PATRON OF PULP LITERATURE

By supporting *Pulp Literature* on Patreon with $2 or more per month, you will be laying the foundation for a secure future for the magazine, as well as ensuring that you never miss an issue! Your subscription includes four big issues of short stories, novellas, poetry, comics, and novel excerpts, delivered to your door or electronic mailbox each year. **Find us at patreon.com/pulplit**

If you prefer to subscribe through our website, go to pulpliterature. com/subscribe.

Or you can send a cheque with the form below to
Subscriptions, Pulp Literature Press, 21955 16 Ave, Langley BC, V2Z 1K5, Canada

Don't miss an issue!

❏ **Send me 2 years (8 issues) at the special rate of $90** (save $30)*
❏ **Send me 1 year (4 issues) for $50** (save $10)*
❏ **Send me 2 years of digital issues for $30** (save $9.92)
❏ **Send me 1 year of digital issues for $17.50** (save $2.47)

Name: ____

Address: ____

City: ________________________________ Prov. / State: _________

Postal code: ______________ Country: ___________________

Email: ____

❏ Payment enclosed   Make cheques payable in Canadian funds to Pulp Literature
❏ Bill me   Press. Include email address for digital editions and Paypal
❏ New   billing, or subscribe at www.pulpliterature.com.
❏ Renewal   *for postage outside Canada add $20 per year in North America or $36 per year overseas.